"How is by

Zaac leaned in to get a better look at her face, but the movement brought him close enough that Miriam could smell his faint scent mingled with hay from the stables.

"Um, she's good," Miriam said. "I changed her diaper, and she has a bottle of milk in her. She seems happiest close by the fire."

"She'll be okay," Zaac said, cocking his head to one side and smiling at the baby.

"*Yah*, I think so."

Zaac cast Miriam a half smile, and she felt a rush of comfort at that smile. She dropped her gaze. She had to stop that. This was her late husband's brother—complication enough. But more than that— he was on his way out of the community. He wasn't her comfort.

Her ex-Amish uncle and her late husband's brother, who seemed inclined to go English, were both here at the same time... Miriam truly believed that *Gott*'s hand was in everything. So what was *Gott* doing?

Patricia Johns is a *Publishers Weekly* bestselling author who writes from Alberta, Canada, where she lives with her husband and son. She writes Amish romances that will leave you yearning for a simpler life. You can find her at patriciajohns.com and on social media, where she loves to connect with her readers. Drop by her website and you might find your next read!

Books by Patricia Johns

Love Inspired

Amish Chocolate Shop Brides

An Amish Baby in Her Arms

Amish Country Matches

The Amish Matchmaking Dilemma
Their Amish Secret
The Amish Marriage Arrangement
An Amish Mother for His Child
Her Pretend Amish Beau
Amish Sleigh Bells

Redemption's Amish Legacies

The Nanny's Amish Family
A Precious Christmas Gift
Wife on His Doorstep
Snowbound with the Amish Bachelor
Blended Amish Blessings
The Amish Matchmaker's Choice

Harlequin Heartwarming

An Amish Antiques Shop Romance

Her Amish Country Husband

Visit the Author Profile page at LoveInspired.com for more titles.

AN AMISH BABY
IN HER ARMS

PATRICIA JOHNS

LOVE INSPIRED
INSPIRATIONAL ROMANCE

LOVE INSPIRED®

LOVE INSPIRED®
INSPIRATIONAL ROMANCE

ISBN-13: 978-1-335-62101-6

An Amish Baby in Her Arms

Copyright © 2025 by Patricia Johns

Love Inspired
22 Adelaide St. West, 41st Floor
Toronto, Ontario M5H 4E3, Canada
www.LoveInspired.com

Printed in Lithuania

Recycling programs
for this product may
not exist in your area.

MIX
Paper | Supporting
responsible forestry
FSC® C021394

Pleasant words are as an honeycomb,
sweet to the soul, and health to the bones.
—*Proverbs* 16:24

To my husband and our son.
You are the center of my world. I love you!

Chapter One

Miriam listened to the roaring thunder and the slap of rain against the glass windows of the Black Bonnet Amish Chocolates shop. She had made a batch of chocolate-covered sea-salt caramels, and the sweet scent of the confections curled through the shop darkened by the storm.

This shop was owned by Esther Mae, and she had a repertoire of chocolate recipes that were tried and true, but Miriam had a few ideas for new chocolate flavors she was eager to try out. Esther Mae had made no promises, but she'd said she'd be happy to taste anything Miriam came up with, and that was an exciting thought. For the first time in a long time, Miriam was thinking hopeful thoughts about the future again.

Miriam's late husband's brother, Isaac Yoder, stood with his weight on one foot, his lips moving as he counted up the money from the day's sales.

"Twenty-eight fives…" Zaac murmured, writing with a ballpoint pen and then picking up the last pile of ones. While Zaac's aunt was away, Miriam and Zaac had been left to run the shop on their own, with Zaac in charge. There had been tension between her and Zaac for years. It had started just before she married Elijah, and that tension had carried on through the short eight months of her marriage, past Elijah's death a year ago, past her miscarriage shortly after that...

Wind whistled past the gutters and rattled them dangerously. Miriam shivered, and Zaac glanced up at her, his dark gaze locking onto her for a moment before he turned back to the pile of bills.

"You should head home," he said, tucking the bundle of cash into a canvas bank deposit bag. "That storm is terrible."

Miriam lived with her grandfather. Her parents had passed away several years ago, and with all her recent heartbreak, living with Dawdie had been the best choice, and Dawdie had been very happy to have her there with him.

The sound of a child's cry wound with the wind past the window, and Miriam's heart squeezed painfully. A year after losing her pregnancy, she still felt like she heard babies crying when there weren't any. When would that stop?

Zaac looked up, frowning. Wait... Had he heard it, too? Miriam's heart skipped a beat. The hiccuping cry of a tiny baby filtered through the howling wind again, and Miriam's heart hammered to a stop. That wasn't some phantom sound from her own heartbreak.

"That sounded like a baby," Miriam breathed.

Zaac straightened. "Where did it come from?"

Miriam went to the window and shaded her eyes to look out the rain-clouded glass. A small car's headlights broke through the downpour as it pulled away from the curb and drove off. Most shops on this street had closed down early, so it was surprising to see anyone out there.

Miriam went over to the front door of the shop and pulled it open. The bell above tinkled cheerfully. There was a rush of wet, rain-scented air that pushed her cape dress back against her legs, and Miriam's gaze dropped to a rather battered-looking car seat placed on the front mat. It was covered with a dirty blanket. Miriam squatted and pulled aside the fabric and inside was a tiny baby wrapped in a soiled receiving blanket—as dirty as the one covering it—the little mouth open in a wail, cheeks wet with tears and eyes scrunched shut.

Miriam's breath caught in her throat, and she picked up the car seat and brought it inside. A tiny baby—the very last reminder she needed on this miserable, cold night. She used her hip to close the door, and the baby's cries filled the shop. The blanket was damp, and the infant had to be freezing cold. Tucked next to the baby was a rain-spattered note, written on the back of a local menu for a fish-and-chips restaurant.

Miriam put the car seat down on the counter and fiddled with the buckles until she could lift the baby free and snuggle the little one close against her. The baby wriggled with a surprising amount of strength, and Miriam smoothed a hand over the downy, dark brown hair that covered the child's soft head. Zaac snatched up the note and smoothed it.

"It says, 'I can't take care of her. Her name is Ivy. Please be kind to her. I can't be her mother…'" Zaac read, and his gaze flickered up at her uncomfortably.

Had that been the car that had driven off? Miriam carried the baby back to the window and looked out. It was hard to see anything through the downpour.

"Is there a bottle or anything?" Miriam asked. The crying baby needed something in her stomach. Someone had dropped her off hungry? Who would do that?

They both looked around, but there was nothing—no bottle, no diapers. Miriam set the baby up on her shoulder and gently tapped her back, but little Ivy pulled her knees up and squirmed, turning her face toward Miriam's neck— a sure and certain sign of hunger. Could she maybe give the baby some cream from the kitchen? But something inside her said no, that wouldn't be the right choice.

"She looks almost newborn," Miriam said past the lump in her throat. "She's smaller than my nephew when he was born, and he was just over six pounds."

Ivy was a tiny little thing, all arms and legs stretching out in frustration and a searching little mouth the size of a grape. Ivy scrunched her face up once more and started to cry all over again, her little chest heaving with each sucked-in breath. She cried as if she'd been crying for hours, and that thought gave Miriam's heart a squeeze.

"Okay…okay…" Zaac looked outside. "I'm going to run up to the police station. That's probably our safest bet. You stay here with the baby, and I'll be back."

Zaac pushed his hat firmly onto his head, grabbed his coat and pushed outside into the rain. The door shut with a bang.

Miriam jiggled the baby gently against her chest, but Ivy cried on. Of all the nights for a tiny baby to arrive on the doorstep, this was the worst! Not only was it cold outside, but this was gearing up to be the worst storm in a long, long while.

Miriam checked the baby's diaper—which was mostly dry. She took a little bit of sugar on her finger and let the baby suck on it. She was hungry, and Miriam knew well enough not to give the infant straight cow's milk. It wouldn't be enough nutrition for her. But wasn't something better than nothing? The baby's cries had subsided, but she was sucking hungrily on the tip of Miriam's finger, and everything inside Miriam longed to feed this little thing. In some aching part of her heart, it was like the baby she'd lost was finally in her arms.

She couldn't let herself feel this way!

This wasn't her baby. This was another woman's baby, and that woman had abandoned her, hungry and crying, in the middle of a storm.

Miriam carried Ivy into the back kitchen, where her fresh batch of sea-salt caramels waited under clean dish towels, and pulled out two thick kitchen towels. She threw the soiled blanket into a laundry hamper and wrapped little Ivy up in the clean towels, then headed back to the front of the store.

The door opened again and Zaac came back inside, dripping water all over the floor.

"They're closed up tight!" he said. "They put a sign out that says to call 911 for emergencies. We'll have to wait until after the storm. What do we do?"

There was no telephone in the chocolate shop. Esther Mae had never installed one even though the bishop permitted it, preferring to take orders face to face.

"I have baby supplies at home," Miriam said.

Zaac met her gaze, and he winced. For just a moment, she saw a flood of compassion in his eyes. "Right. Of course."

She'd been getting ready for her own child's arrival a year ago and hadn't relinquished any of the supplies she'd gathered. But more recently, she had been babysitting for her sister's new baby boy. There was a can of newborn formula still in a cupboard. They had baby items enough.

"Okay, then we're set." Zaac gave a curt not. "This isn't against the law, is it? I mean...we're not kidnapping or anything?"

"The baby was dropped off on our doorstep, and we can't contact the local police," Miriam said. "What else are we supposed to do?"

What did you do when an Englisher left a newborn baby on your doorstep—in the middle of a raging storm, no less?

"I think you're right," he said. "After the storm you can contact the police, right? We aren't getting to the bank for the deposit tonight either. Let's just put the money under the counter. I'm sure Aent Esther Mae will understand."

"You don't mind driving me home?" she asked. She'd planned to ask for a ride with a friend, but it would be better to have Zaac drive her.

"Do you really think I'm the kind of man who'd leave you to figure out a ride home with a baby in your arms?"

She wasn't sure what she thought of him, except that he'd always seemed to be glaring at her before she married Elijah. "You'd best hitch up quickly, then," Miriam said. "This baby needs to eat."

"I'll be quick about it," Zaac said.

Ten minutes later, Zaac had his buggy in front of the store, and little Ivy was crying plaintively again, one thin arm waving around as if she could somehow find what she was looking for.

Why had that mother simply left her newborn? Was she in trouble? Was she struggling with something like addiction and knew that her baby would be safer with another family? Miriam knew what it felt like to be a mother without a baby in her arms, and the tragedy of this situation was not lost on her. That mother would mourn this, one way or another. There was no way not to grieve the loss of a child. But one thing was clear—Ivy's mother had given her up.

"It's okay, Ivy," Miriam said softly, rocking the wailing baby back and forth. "I'll take care of you. I've got you, sweetie."

And for the next little while, she did. She would stand in for Ivy's mother until they could get her into loving, responsible arms again.

Oh, Gott, let that be soon... Because she wasn't sure how long her poor aching heart could take this.

Miriam stood by the window and watched as Zaac jumped down from his buggy and came hurrying over to the front door. She stepped outside and hunched over the baby as a swirl of rain whipped around them. Zaac used Esther Mae's keys to lock up, and then he opened up an umbrella and held it over Miriam's head as they rushed toward the buggy.

Zaac struggled with the umbrella against the gusting wind, and Miriam kept her head down. When they got to the buggy, Zaac put a strong hand under her elbow and helped boost her up. Her stomach fluttered at his strength. It brought too strong a reminder of Elijah, and Zaac's disapproving look. Zaac closed the door after her, and she looked down at the baby's scrunched little face. Ivy's hair was dark and damp, and when she opened her eyes just a little, Miriam could make out their brilliant blue. She pressed a soft kiss against the baby girl's forehead.

"Gott, protect this baby," Miriam prayed softly. "She needs you."

And may Gott speed this storm by.

Zaac climbed up in the driver's seat of his buggy and slammed his door shut against the driving rain. He looked over at Miriam, her face flushed from the cold rain and the baby snuggled close against her chest, and his heart gave a tumble...just like it always did. She didn't think too much of him, and maybe he understood that. He'd never thought his brother's marriage was a good idea, and he'd even suggested that Elijah not marry her at all. He stood by that.

But not because Miriam wasn't wonderful. His brother hadn't been worthy of *her*! Elijah wasn't a reliable man, and wedding vows hadn't changed a thing. Going out drinking with friends and driving his buggy while inebriated...that had been the cause of the buggy accident that killed Elijah and left Miriam a widow. And yet, for all Elijah's flaws, he'd still been his little brother, and Zaac missed him.

Zaac untied Schon's reins and leaned forward to make sure the road was clear. Then he released the tension in the reins and Schon started forward, pulling them into the street. The gelding's head was down against the driving rain, but he was strong and sure.

"I doubt we can open the store again until this storm passes," Zaac said, squinting against the rain-coated windshield. Sometimes there was a choice to make between staying dry with the sliding window shut and seeing the road with the window open.

"Esther Mae normally stays closed during storms like this one," Miriam replied. "She thinks it's better to stay safe, and will be glad we left early. Besides, not many tourists will be out shopping during this kind of storm."

"Hmm." He nodded. His *aent* was a good businesswoman. She'd been running this shop ever since her husband died, and that had been when Zaac was about five—young enough that he didn't remember more than his first view of a coffin. So for all the time that Zaac could recall, Aent Esther Mae had been making her chocolates and selling them.

"I'm really grateful you were here to drive us, but can I ask why you wanted to do this?" Miriam asked.

"Do what?" he asked.

"Run the shop," she said. "You've never worked in the shop—not for years, at least."

He glanced over at Miriam. Even he knew that Miriam would have been a better choice than him for the job, but this had been a special favor.

"I need the experience," he replied. "I want to be able to apply for some ranch-managing positions."

He reined Schon in at a four-way stop and waited while a pickup truck passed in front of them. Then he released the reins again, and they started forward.

"I thought if I could get some management experience, it might help me find some other work that would let me live on-site at a ranch. Aent Esther Mae was helping me get some more experience to help with that."

"Do you want to move away from home?" she asked.

"*Yah*. I do."

"Won't your *mamm* miss you?"

"She has my sisters at home, and Johannes is helping on the ranch now. I know he and my sister would be happy to move in and take over the ranch if I wasn't there to do it. Besides, if I make a good enough wage, I can send money back to her."

This was more than he'd admitted to anyone. Even Aent Esther Mae only knew that he wanted a better-paying job, not that he wanted to live away from home. There was more to his decision that he wasn't ready to share yet.

He glanced toward his late brother's wife. She held the baby close, her cheek against the infant's head. The baby was still crying, but less desperately. Miriam's touch seemed to be comforting for the little thing. Miriam's eyes suddenly misted, and Zaac's heart clenched in response. She had gone through a lot in the last year, and he'd always felt this protective tenderness toward her…even when it hadn't been appropriate. He still shouldered that guilt—another good reason to start over elsewhere. Because while his brother had been married to Miriam, Zaac had been harboring some very tender feelings for her, too. That hadn't been right! He should never have allowed himself to feel more for Miriam than friendliness, but he could see a depth to Miriam's character that his brother couldn't. He could see her earnestness and her good intentions. And he could see when Elijah had hurt her feelings, too…

Zaac pushed that back. That was more than a year ago now. He'd felt far too much for Miriam, and he wasn't going to make any excuses for himself. The difference was, Zaac would never cross that line. She'd chosen Elijah, and he'd accepted that. There was right and there was wrong, and while Elijah had blurred those lines, Zaac never would.

The Smucker farm was located a twenty-minute buggy ride from town, but it took a good thirty-five to get there in this blowing gale. There were a few buggies out still, but he didn't even bother squinting through the rain to see who was passing by. It was the cars and trucks that worried him. The visibility was so low that this was a dangerous drive—one that brought to mind the tangled remains of his brother's buggy. Again, he shoved back the memories. Maybe if he moved farther away, he would leave some of those wrenching memories behind, too.

When they finally turned down the Smuckers' drive, sheltered somewhat by the trees lining the way, Zaac's anxiety was under control again. The baby was still crying, but it was a softer cry now. The best thing that Zaac could do was get Miriam and the infant into the house. Kerosene lights were glowing on the bottom floor, and a puff of smoke was visible in the chimney, the cloud whisked away as quickly as it appeared by the buffeting winds.

Zaac pulled up as close to the door as he could get. A red pickup truck was parked by the stable, and he spared it a curious glance. Then he jumped out of the buggy, went up the steps and pounded loudly on the side door, leaving Miriam in the buggy until he could clear a straight path for her inside. He didn't bother with the umbrella for himself—it was just a battle against the wind, anyway.

The door opened after a moment, and he was met by Miriam's grandfather, Obie. The old man squinted at him.

"Zaac? Have you seen Miriam? She's supposed to be on her way. I've been worried sick!"

Rain poured off the edge of Zaac's hat, and his shoulders were already soaked through, water dripping down his back and his chest.

"She's with me," Zaac said, raising his voice to be heard over the howling wind. "She's in the buggy. There's an umbrella in there. The thing is, someone left a newborn baby on the doorstep at the shop, and we've brought her back here. There was no other choice. I know it's an inconvenience, but—"

"A baby?" Obie asked with a frown, and he planted his hat on his head and reached for his coat.

Another man appeared behind him—Obie's son, Elmer. He was in his late forties and dressed in Englisher clothes, with an Englisher beard that included a mustache, but Zaac recognized him. That would explain the truck. Elmer had left the Amish faith twenty years ago, but he'd come back to visit often enough, and people talked about him so that Zaac knew him by sight.

"Hi, Elmer. It's good to see you."

"Sorry, you're—"

"This is Isaac Yoder," Obie said irritably. "Well, let's get Miriam and the little one inside. Elmer, stoke up the fire a bit, would you?"

Obie snatched a shawl off a hook and marched out into the deluge. Even in his eighties, he was tough.

Zaac followed and pulled out the umbrella again. The wind immediately whipped it inside out, and Zaac muttered his frustration and tossed it into the back of the buggy. Obie pulled out the shawl and wrapped it around both Miriam and the baby, then hurried her from the buggy into the house.

"Come on in," Obie called over his shoulder to Zaac.

Zaac guided Schon past the truck and underneath the buggy shelter, which provided a solid roof and some walls to stop the wind and rain from battering the poor horse.

"I won't be long," he murmured.

By the time Zaac got to the door, he was dripping wet again. He could feel a rivulet running down his legs from where his pants touched his skin, giving an entry point for the moisture. The sky suddenly lit up with a flickering array of lightning, forking across the sky. There was a heartbeat of anticipation, and then an earth-shattering boom. Zaac opened the door and slammed it shut behind him. A welcoming rush of warm air met him.

"Here…" Elmer tossed him a dry towel, and Zaac nodded his thanks, using it to mop some of the water off his face and hair. He hadn't been in the Smucker home since the last time the family had hosted Service Sunday. Never as a regular guest.

Miriam stood by the stove, shivering, her dress not quite as soaked as it would have been if her grandfather hadn't brought her a shawl. Ivy wailed in spite of the warmth—so hungry she could probably think of little else. Obie stood at the counter with a can of formula and a baby bottle. He was soaked through, too, but his hat had protected his thinning gray hair.

"Just one little scoop, Dawdie, and fill it up with water to the line on the bottle," Miriam said as she gently bobbed Ivy up and down to comfort her.

Obie squinted at the bottle, making a face of concentration as he looked at the bottle.

"Here…" Zaac said. "My eyes might be better."

Obie shot him a look of annoyance. "I can see just fine, Isaac."

Then he squinted again at the bottle, moving it farther away and then closer. It was clear he wanted no help from Zaac.

"Daet, let me try," Elmer said, and the old man reluctantly released the baby bottle into his son's hands. Elmer filled the bottle to the line, gave it a stir with a clean butter knife, and screwed on the top. He handed it over to Miriam, who adjusted the baby in her arms and popped the nipple into the infant's mouth. The wailing immediately ceased and was replaced by a noisy sucking sound. All of the tension in Miriam's face suddenly smoothed away, and her gentle gaze locked on the baby's face.

"There you are…" Miriam murmured. "Better?"

Zaac felt a wave of relief, too, and he looked over to see Elmer and Obie both with the same relieved expression on their faces.

"We found her on the doorstep," Miriam said, looking up. "We tried to contact the police, but the local station shut down early. What do we do?"

"We can call social services," Elmer said. "Hold on… I'll find a number here somewhere."

He pulled out his phone and typed on it with his thumbs.

Right—Englishers had cell phones and access to all that information at their fingertips. Elmer called a number he found and spoke with someone on the other line while the rest of them waited, listening to the one-sided conversation.

"Do we have enough baby supplies for a couple of days?" Elmer asked.

Miriam nodded.

"They want to know if we can take care of the baby until the storm lifts. They'll send out a social services agent to pick her up as soon as it's safe."

"Of course we can," Miriam said.

Elmer relayed the address of the farm and finished up the call. Zaac's job here was done. Miriam was safe at home with her grandfather and *ankel*. The authorities had been contacted about the baby.

"I'll head out now," Zaac said, nodding toward the door.

There was a shuddering booming sound from the direction of the highway. That wasn't thunder…

"That's an accident." Miriam's voice was close by his shoulder, and he looked down at her in surprise. He hadn't noticed her approach, but the baby's little hands opened and closed in time to her sucking on the bottle.

Together Zaac and Miriam stood in front of the window, squinting in the direction of the highway not far off. There was a smudge of orange light. A fire.

"I don't think Isaac should be driving in this," Elmer said. "How far do you have to drive tonight, young man?"

"Uh…" Zaac looked over at Obie uncomfortably. "Not far. About twenty minutes west."

Elmer shook his head. "Daet, this is how buggy accidents happen." His gaze flicked toward Miriam sympathetically. "Thank Gott he got Miriam home, but I would feel wrong about letting this young man take his buggy out in this storm. I'm still waiting on the mechanic for my truck, so I can't even drive him myself. But these roads are dangerous. We know that better than most, don't we?"

Considering the accident that had killed Zaac's brother. The older man's meaning was clear between the lines. They had all learned firsthand how devastating an accident could be. But Zaac didn't need their pity, either.

Obie softened then. "True."

"I'm not asking to stay here," Zaac interjected. He'd make the effort to go home with a prayer and some good intentions.

"I know, I know," Obie said. "But my son is right. Those roads are not safe. Besides, that accident on the highway is going to block off traffic until at least tomorrow. I don't see any other choice. You're going to have to stay with us. You'd best get your horse into the stable and tie down anything you don't want to blow away in your buggy."

And when Zaac looked down at Miriam with the infant in her arms, she just shrugged, her focus on Ivy as she drained the bottle down to white frothy bubbles.

"No choice," Miriam murmured.

Yah, he would have to agree—there was no choice now. But that didn't mean Miriam would like it. Zaac would only stay as long as he absolutely had to, and then he'd head home.

Chapter Two

❧

"It's good to see you again," the Englisher man said, holding out a hand.

Elmer wore a pair of blue jeans and cowboy boots, and a T-shirt with a church mission logo on it and the tagline "Go tell it on the mountain." That was from a song that the Amish didn't sing, but Zaac recognized it from going to church with some non-Amish friends. Other denominations were quite different from what Zaac was used to. But it had gotten him thinking lately about the things they should be doing.

"Likewise," Zaac said, shaking his hand. "I haven't seen you since…" He swallowed. "Since my brother's funeral, I guess."

A lot of people had come for Elijah's funeral—their family from near and far, and Miriam's family, too. Even her Englisher *ankel* and *aent* had come. It had been a miserable, sad day, but there had been a lot of loving support.

"*Yah*. That would be it." Elmer cast him a sympathetic look. "Let me help you out with your horse. Two of us will get it done faster in that storm."

"*Danke*, I appreciate it," Zaac replied.

The sooner Zaac got Schon into the warm, dry stable, the sooner he could dry off and warm up, too. Miriam moved closer to the stove again. Ivy had finished her bottle, and she put the baby up onto her shoulder to burp her. Obie bent to push another stick of wood into the stove.

Zaac would stay one night. His mother would be worried when he didn't make it home tonight, but she also knew that he wouldn't endanger himself unnecessarily. He looked over at Elmer hopefully.

"Do you think I could use your phone?" Zaac asked. "I'd like to call my *mamm*'s Englisher neighbor and let him know where I am. If she worries about me, she'll check in next door, and at least she'll know I'm okay."

"*Yah*, of course." Elmer fished the phone out of his pocket and handed it over.

Zaac left the message and returned the phone, and then they both pulled on some extra coats that were hanging by the door and plunged outside into the storm. At least his mother wouldn't worry as much now. She'd already lost one son to an accident, and he knew exactly where her mind would go when he didn't come back tonight.

The rain was coming down in a torrent, and the downspouts were pouring out a steady gush of rainwater that turned the grass beyond into a marsh. Lightning flashed, forking across the sky, and then there was a teeth-rattling boom. Zaac ducked his head, using his hat to shield his face against the driving rain as he and Elmer headed toward the buggy shelter together.

Schon waited under the shelter, his coat trembling with each crash of thunder. His ears twitched, and Zaac's heart went out to the poor horse. He put a reassuring hand on the animal's shoulder, then stroked his neck.

"I told you I'd be back," he murmured. "You doing okay, Schon?"

The horse shuffled his hooves, and Zaac started working

on the buckles to get him unhitched. Elmer joined Zaac on the other side, and together they worked on getting the animal out of the harness.

"I'm sorry about your brother's passing," Elmer said, raising his voice to be heard over the storm. "How have you and your family been holding up?"

"We're doing better now," Zaac said. "Some days are better than others, though."

"I'm glad you were looking out for my niece tonight."

"Of course. As long as I'm around, I'll look out for her."

Which was partly why he needed space. He'd keep looking out for her—he wouldn't be able to help himself. And it would be an unhealthy balance. Miriam was a woman who had never been loved well enough, and who deserved so much better than she'd gotten in her short marriage to Elijah. She was also a woman who would never approve of the next step Zaac was planning to take—to leave home and their community behind him.

The two men lifted the collar off Schon's head, and Zaac led the horse away from the buggy now that he was free. A flash of lightning made the horse startle, though, and Zaac kept a firm hold on the bridle.

"I'll get the door," Elmer said, hurrying ahead to open the stable door. The wind surged once more before the heavy door slid open, and they stepped inside the warm stable. Schon's hooves clopped against the cement floor, and he nickered, shaking his head.

Elmer pulled the door shut behind them and brought out some matches to light a kerosene lamp hanging overhead. He cupped his hand around the flame to protect it, and then the lamp flared to life, illuminating the small, clean stable. Elmer shook out the match, licked his fingers and damped the ember.

Three stalls had horses already lodged inside, but a fourth sat empty. Zaac got a towel and began to dry the horse off.

Having some time alone with the ex-Amish rancher was actually a gift. Zaac had questions…if he got up the courage to ask them.

"How are things going for you, Elmer?" he asked. "How is your ranch faring?"

"It's going very well." Elmer shot him a good-natured smile. "We have about five thousand acres that we're working."

"How did you do that?" Zaac asked. "I mean…you bought it?"

"We bought the first plot of land ourselves, and then my wife Trish's uncle was selling his section of land about five years ago, and so we bought that at a really fair price. Then we picked up another section right up against it a year after for a steal, and we went from there. One family farm blossomed into a good-sized cattle ranch now, and we sell beef for market and rent out some sire bulls."

Zaac let out a low whistle. "You must have employees working that size of a ranch, then."

"*Yah*, of course. I had to learn the hard way about what makes for a good worker, I can tell you that!"

"Is your wife running the ranch while you're away?"

"She's in Wyoming visiting her family. I've got a ranch manager. It's a pretty big operation. He's put in his notice, though. I've got another three weeks until he's gone. It was now or never to come back and see my *daet*."

Zaac's heart skipped a beat. He was stuck on the fact that Elmer was losing his ranch manager. "So…you're looking for a replacement?"

"*Yah*, sure am."

Elmer headed over to a large bale of hay, the top of

a pile of three, and its twine was already cut. He pulled off a flake of the bale and passed it to Zaac who put it in Schon's feeder.

Zaac grabbed the water bucket hanging on the side of the stall and headed over to a tap to fill it. He didn't want to push too hard or say the wrong thing, but this seemed like an awfully good opportunity—exactly the kind of opportunity Zaac had been praying for. Could Gott be working through this storm?

"I'm looking for a job just like that," Zaac said.

"Oh, well, this isn't an Amish ranch," Elmer said. "There's a fair amount of electronics involved. Plus tractors, and we wrangle the cattle on four wheelers. I'm not sure this is the kind of place the bishop would approve of, honestly."

"I understand that, but it wouldn't be a problem for me." Zaac straightened. "I'm planning on leaving the community."

"Oh." Elmer sobered. "Are you leaving the faith, too, or just going to a more liberal settlement?"

"I'm leaving the Amish life completely." This was the first time he'd admitted it out loud to anyone, and his heart gave a sad squeeze. There was a lot that he'd miss about Menno Hills, and about the Amish life in general. But his conscience had been stinging him. This wasn't about his comfort, because if it were, he'd stay Amish.

Elmer nodded slowly, his gaze fixed on Zaac with an uncomfortable directness, and Zaac found himself talking to fill the silence—and perhaps defend himself a little bit, too.

"I wanted to make sure I had enough experience and a good job lined up before I made the move," Zaac went on. "My *aent* is letting me get some management experience in her chocolate shop, and I'm hoping that running a ranch of our own, combined with some other manage-ment experience, might be enough to recommend me for a position like that."

Elmer chewed the inside of his cheek. "You aren't very old, Isaac."

"I've got work experience."

"Managing a ranch like mine is a much bigger opera-tion than a chocolate shop."

"I know it is," Zaac said, "but a man has to start some-where. I've always liked that part of scripture where Moses was scared to go back to Egypt, and Gott told him to look at what he had in his hand. Moses had a staff—and Gott used that staff. And I'd like to do just that—work with what I've got in my hand and ask Gott to bless it. And what I've got is ranching experience the Amish way, and an oppor-tunity to learn about leadership in a retail store. I know they don't normally combine, but I think they could this time. I'm looking for work where my skills and experience can be an asset."

Elmer pursed his lips. "I admire your attitude—I do. I also think you'll find yourself a good position somewhere, but you might want to start lower as a ranch hand. You could even get into horse training and start out as a loper. Mechanics are always in demand, but that would mean going back to school a bit. It's different out in the rest of the country, Isaac. It's not the same. How old are you?"

"Twenty-two," he replied.

"*Yah.* That's the thing. Out in the rest of America, you're still considered a kid."

But not in the Amish world. In an Amish community, Zaac was plenty old enough to get married and have some *kinner* of his own. Elijah had been a year younger when he'd died, and he'd been married with a baby on the way.

"I'm eager to start my life," Zaac said.

He was eager to get away from the memories, away from the guilt associated with his feelings for Miriam and away from the chaffing of his conscience where he was certain the Amish were wrong.

"Look, I don't mean to discourage you," Elmer said. "The truth is, if I help you jump the fence, there's going to be a lot of blowback for me. It's one thing to leave on my own, and quite another to help young people leave the community. I told myself I would never do that. I'm sorry."

Zaac's heart sank. He'd hoped that this was Gott bringing the right opportunity his way, but maybe it wasn't.

"Do you know anyone who might be hiring?" he asked.

"Not at the moment, but if I hear of something I can let you know."

"*Danke.* I would be grateful," Zaac replied. A job was a job, and he'd be grateful for what he could get.

What did Zaac have in his hand right now? One connection with an ex-Amish rancher who might be able to help him find employment. He had his own ranching experience and his *aent*'s help in learning to manage a shop.

Maybe it didn't add up to as much as he had hoped.

Miriam stood on a step stool in the storage room and pulled down the various sizes of cloth diapers she had on hand. She hadn't bought any newborn-size ones yet. She'd been waiting—most times, a new *mamm* could borrow diapers from other women in the community. She stopped, her hand on the soft cloth, her heart in her throat.

A year ago, she was getting ready for her own baby, and sometimes that fact hit her harder than others. Like now.

Oh, Gott...why did you bring a baby to my door? she prayed. *I was moving on!*

She'd been able to go whole workdays without thinking about her loss. She'd been focusing on a new future—the kind that Esther Mae had, with a business of her own and a warm, solid connection to her Amish community. Miriam didn't want to marry again. Marriage had been incredibly difficult. But she could pursue other interests, like candy making. She'd found herself actually happy again, trying new combinations in the kitchen.

But from the other room, she heard Ivy's fussing cry. She needed out of that diaper and into something clean and dry. There wasn't time for her own grief, and Miriam felt the unfairness of that, too. There was another baby in her home, needing love, and milk, and diapers… There was another baby needing mothering.

Miriam shook out one of the folded white diaper cloths from babysitting her nephew, and the cloth was bigger than Ivy! She folded it over a couple of times. It wasn't going to fit, no matter how hard she tried. But there was a solution to this.

Miriam took another couple of cloth diapers under her arm and headed back out to the kitchen. Dawdie sat in a chair a few feet from the stove, the baby up on his shoulder as he gently patted her back. She continued to fuss.

"I need the scissors," Miriam said, and she pulled open a kitchen drawer. All she had to do was make the cloth smaller, and she could fold the diapers for this tiny baby. This little girl deserved a diaper that fit her.

Dawdie's gaze moved toward the window, and he pressed his lips together in a tight line.

"How do you feel about Isaac being here?" he asked.

Miriam cut through the fabric with the heavy scissors, taking a few inches off each side. How did she feel? A little anxious, honestly.

"I don't have much choice," she said instead.

"It isn't right to hold a grudge, Miriam."

"Dawdie, he tried to stop my wedding," Miriam said. "He told Elijah not to marry me. That is hard to get over. I can forgive him—my husband is dead and buried. But I still remember."

She spread out a blanket on the kitchen table and then put a receiving blanket on top of that one, then took little Ivy and laid her on top of that. She worked quickly, removing the old disposable diaper Ivy had worn for far too long, and using a soft, wet cloth to clean her up.

"For yourself, Miriam, you should try to put it behind you," Dawdie said. "I know—I was hesitant, too. But I'm feeling rather impressed by Gott to forgive and put it behind us. We are all moving forward. Now, I'm going to go on upstairs and find something dry for Isaac to wear."

Dawdie really was intent on forgiving Zaac, and it was to her grandfather's credit. Miriam would if she could, and Gott knew that she'd tried. But then she'd remember the stories Elijah had told her, how Zaac didn't think she was good enough for Elijah. And she had been a good wife! She'd loved her husband dearly, and she'd done her best to be a blessing to him. Zaac's judgment of her had not been fair, and it had been downright cruel of him to attempt to dissuade Elijah from marrying her.

Miriam turned back to the baby as Dawdie went up the staircase. This storm had locked Miriam in with Zaac… and maybe she would find forgiving him a little bit easier if his attempt to stop the wedding hadn't almost worked! Elijah had very nearly broken up with her—convinced that his brother was right and the wedding was a bad idea. If Elijah had brushed his brother's comments aside, maybe she could brush aside the slight. But it was all tangled up in a large amount of pain.

Marriage might not have been easy, but she had loved her husband.

Gott, please take away my anger, she prayed silently. *Just wipe it out of my heart completely.*

Miriam had begun sewing *bobbli* clothes for her child. She had an infant dress already made, and she found it in a basket and shook it out. She'd meant to keep this dress as a reminder of the child she lost, but it was cold, and this baby needed more than a blanket.

Miriam carefully pulled the dress onto Ivy's wriggling body, and then wrapped a fresh, warm blanket around her. She blinked up at Miriam with those big blue eyes, and her heart ached afresh. Such a tiny baby left on a doorstep... and here was Miriam, who'd wanted her child with all her heart, and this little one was wearing the *bobbli* dress of the child she'd lost. It wasn't fair. But the rain fell on the just and the unjust, the Good Book said. Sometimes life just happened, and that was no comfort at all.

"I'd keep you forever if I could," Miriam whispered.

Miriam's life had not turned out like she'd expected. She'd thought she was starting on her own houseful of *kinner* to love and raise to be good and honest youngsters. And now, she'd buried her husband, lost her baby and she was left with only a prayer in her heart that Gott would provide.

The baby nuzzled into Miriam's neck. With one hand, Miriam cleared the blankets off the table as she heard the side door into the mudroom open. The mudroom was closed off from the rest of the kitchen with another door that shut tight. It helped to keep the house warmer in winter when they didn't lose all that heat every time the side door opened.

She heard the sound of boots and the faucet turning on while the men washed up. Their voices, while pitched low, carried through to the kitchen.

"You'd need to get a cell phone to start," Elmer was saying. "People have to be able to reach you easily."

"We have the neighbor—"

"*Yah*, but that's for some rare time someone might need to find you, right?" Elmer's voice was stronger. "If you're looking for work, they need to contact you about interviews, about your schedule. A ranch manager would be the one calling employees about schedule changes, so you need to be reachable."

Ankel Elmer was suggesting that Zaac get a cell phone? That went directly against their Ordnung! Elmer knew how things worked here. People in these parts accommodated the Amish ways. They understood that it was a matter of conscience. Didn't they? At the very least, Ankel Elmer should!

"How much does it cost to own a car?" Zaac asked.

"There's the cost of the car, which can cost more if you want a newer, more reliable vehicle. How much do you know about mechanics?"

Silence.

"You might want to put more money into a newer car, then. Plus, there's insurance and gas. I'm thinking monthly, it's about…"

Miriam stood in silence, her breath bated. Was it wrong to be listening? They obviously thought this was a private conversation. They murmured back and forth a little bit, and then Elmer concluded, "I can give you a bit of advice on things like that, but I really can't help more than that. You understand?"

"I do. I appreciate the advice, all the same."

Ivy whined and started to squirm, and the voices in the mudroom silenced. Miriam patted the baby's back and moved closer to the stove as the mudroom door opened and the men came back inside.

Was Zaac really considering jumping the fence? Why would he do that? Ankel Elmer had left the faith for his wife. That was what she'd been told, at least, even though it was before her time. So did Zaac have a girlfriend out there? Someone luring him away from the Plain life?

"I'm freezing," Zaac said as he came out of the mudroom. "Do you mind if I share that stove with you, Miriam?"

"Feel free," Miriam said. "Ankel Elmer, how are you?"

"I'm a bit damp, but not too bad," Elmer replied. "I'll start a pot of coffee. That should be welcome right about now."

Elmer headed into the kitchen to fetch the coffee fixings himself, and Zaac joined her at the woodstove, holding his cold-reddened hands out toward the heat. His clothes were sodden, and he'd left wet footprints from his sock feet across the wooden floor. His hair was damp, too.

"Dawdie is getting you some dry clothes to wear," Miriam said.

"That'll help," he said, and she noticed some goose bumps on his arm where the sleeve was pushed up. He was cold.

"How is Ivy doing?" he asked, and he leaned closer to get a better look at her face, but the movement brought him in close enough that she could smell his faint musky scent mingling with the hay from the stable.

"Um, she's good," Miriam said, and she tried not to

notice the manly scent that lingered on Zaac's clothing. "I changed her diaper, and she has a bottle of formula in her. She seems happiest close by the fire."

"She'll be okay," Zaac said, cocking his head to one side and smiling at the baby.

"*Yah*, I think so."

Zaac cast Miriam a half smile, and she found herself smiling back. She dropped her gaze. She had to stop that.

"I've got some pants and a shirt that should fit you," Dawdie said, coming down the stairs. "The pants might be a little short, but they're dry."

"My clothes might fit him a bit better," Elmer suggested.

Everyone turned and looked at Elmer standing there in his blue jeans and T-shirt.

"Or not," Elmer said with a rueful little smile. "Never mind."

"*Danke*, Obie," Zaac said, and he moved away from the stove, heading over to her grandfather to accept the clothing.

Elijah had died while being rebellious and out of control. He'd been killed while racing a buggy—there were men betting on the outcome, she'd been told. And now Zaac was planning on going English. Maybe the two brothers weren't so different after all. She'd fallen in love with Elijah, and she'd thought that she could somehow fix him, or be his guiding light and his better influence. She'd thought that by marrying her, he was choosing to settle down and leave his more raucous days behind him. Oh, how foolish she had been!

Zaac might be tall and handsome. He might even be charming when he put his mind to it, or when he didn't put his mind to it and was simply being all gruff and considerate. But Miriam was not a fool, and she knew enough to keep her distance this time around. Rebellious men broke hearts, pure and simple. No one knew that better than she did.

Chapter Three

Zaac took the stack of fresh clothes from Obie and headed up the stairs to get changed. Upstairs was considerably colder than downstairs, where the fire was blazing, and he was eager to get these sodden clothes off his body and into something clean and dry.

The first door that was left open a crack was a bedroom, and he slipped inside. There was still daylight coming in through the curtained windows, although it was dim from the deluge out there.

There were three dresses hanging on hooks on the wall. On a little shelf above, he saw two fresh, gauzy *kapps* and a black bonnet sitting stiff and upright. This was Miriam's room, he realized, and he looked around in uncomfortable curiosity.

The bed was neatly made with a block quilt, and he spotted a Bible on the bedside table next to a wind-up clock that was ticking comfortingly into the dimness. This room certainly said something about the woman who kept it. It was clean, neat and simple—Amish perfection.

His brother had been a fool to take Miriam for granted like he had. She was a good woman, and Zaac had done what he could to protect her. It hadn't been enough, though, and that had rankled him. But he'd tried. Zaac might be wanting to leave the faith, but it wasn't because he didn't see the goodness of the Amish life. His reasons were more complicated.

He opened the front of the Bible. On the inside cover, in rolling handwritten script, was written *To our daughter. With love, Mamm and Daet.*

A gift from her late parents. He let the cover close again. Zaac's *mamm* should have taken over for Miriam and been a mother to her, even after Elijah's death. But Elijah had been a difficult husband, and Miriam had seemed more comfortable with her own family. They had all grieved after Elijah's death in the buggy accident, but their grief had taken them all into different corners, and that was part of why it felt so uncomfortable to be here in her home. Even before Elijah died, Zaac hadn't come here to visit her grandfather. They were tied by marriage, but Zaac had known how his brother was treating Miriam, and he'd been racked with guilt about it.

Gott, I need to get home, he prayed silently. *I stayed away for a reason, and I'm afraid that being too close to her will bring back old feelings.*

As if in reply from above, the windows rattled with a gust of pattering rain. The storm was nowhere close to letting up.

Zaac quickly changed out of his wet clothes and into the dry ones Obie had provided. The broadfall pants fit in the waist, but they were short in the leg, and he looked down at four inches of sock-clad ankle that protruded out the bottom. They'd have to do—it was better than being cold. He slipped his arms through his suspenders, gathered up his wet clothes and headed out toward the stairs.

A humored smile turned up Miriam's lips when she saw him on the stairs.

"Those pants are short on you," Miriam said.

"A little," Zaac agreed.

"I can't help that," Obie said irritably. "My legs are of regular length."

Zaac chuckled. "I appreciate the loan of clothing, Obie. Do you have a clothes rack handy?"

Obie went down the basement staircase and emerged a minute later with a folded wire clothes drying rack. He set it up on the far side the stove—still with access to heat, but not in the way—and Zaac laid his wet clothes over the rack to let them dry out.

There was something very sweet about this kitchen— Miriam with the baby cradled in her arms and her grandfather's gruff goodwill. Then there was Elmer, perfectly content to get himself his own coffee. He was hovering over the percolating pot.

Rain drummed on the roof overhead, and Zaac could hear the creaking of a tree's bough outside, the twigs clattering against the kitchen windowpane over the sink with each howling gust. That window overlooked the garden and the barns beyond, and an old, gnarled apple tree grew nearby the house—too close, in Zaac's opinion, but it wasn't exactly his business. It was a surprisingly tall and bushy tree. Whoever had planted that sapling must not have expected such robust results.

"We should probably find a little cradle for the baby," Obie said.

"We don't have one," Miriam said, and her voice shook ever so slightly.

"We left the car seat at the store," Zaac said. It had been a foolish mistake, but he hadn't been thinking.

Elijah had only just found out that he'd be a father when he'd died. Building a cradle would have been Elijah's responsibility. "We could use a basket. There's one with baby blankets inside in the pantry." Her voice shook again.

"Your blankets…" Obie said.

Zaac's heart dropped. The blankets she'd started collecting for the baby she'd lost.

"She's already wrapped in one of them, and I've got her dressed in one of the *bobbli* dresses I sewed. There's a baby here now who needs them," she said, her voice tight. "We could put a folded blanket in the bottom and lay Ivy on top of that. That should be safe. She can't roll out, and it wouldn't be overly soft—that can be a danger, too, you know."

"I'll get it, then," Obie said. "*Danke*, Miriam. This is kind of you." Obie headed down the hallway, and a door squeaked open.

That tree limb outside had drawn Zaac's attention, though—the creaking sound was getting louder, and the twigs and leaves slapped against the glass more forcefully now. The wind moaned as it wound around the chicken coop and the stable.

"I have some muffins made this morning," Miriam said. "I'm sure everyone is getting hungry. I'll get some dinner started, too."

She headed over to the kitchen sink, the baby up on her shoulder in a practiced way that most Amish women had with babies and young children. There were always little ones to be cared for in a growing community, so everyone got a lot of practice. At least, Zaac had with his nieces and nephews. At any family gathering, he'd end up with two or three little kids clinging to him, asking questions or wanting shoulder rides. But the tiny babies normally ended up with one of the girls or women. Zaac's uncles joked that Zaac got to hold his nieces and nephews once they were old enough to bounce. That got laughs from the men who knew it was a joke, and long-suffering looks from the women who didn't care for that kind of wisecracking.

Miriam moved some bars of chocolate aside on the counter, and Zaac couldn't help but follow them with his eyes. She noticed his attention.

"I'm making some chocolate-dipped potato chips later."

"Yah?" He hadn't heard of those.

"I got the idea from the sea-salt caramels," she said. "I think they'd taste good. Sweet and salty combined."

"Maybe a couple of large grains of salt on top of the chocolate," he said.

"Yah." She smiled then, relaxing a little bit. "I think they'd be really good. But I need to try a few different variations. I need to know what's better—sweet white chocolate, milk chocolate or a more bitter dark chocolate. Also, I could layer in some melted peanut butter or butterscotch chips melted down and tempered."

He wasn't sure if she was talking more to herself now than to him, but she did look happy talking about her creations. He used to watch his *aent* make different chocolates, and she'd gotten that same happy look on her face when she was making something new.

"I could taste-test." He was half joking.

"Sure. But you'd have to give me an honest opinion. This matters."

"Are you going to make them for Black Bonnet?" he asked.

"Maybe. If Esther Mae likes them well enough."

He moved closer.

"You really seem happy when you're working with candy," he said.

She shrugged. "I like it. I think I might end up like your *aent*."

"How so?"

"Single, but with a business that brings joy to people."

"Why single?" he asked.

Miriam cast him a flat look. "I've been married. I don't want to do it again."

There was something in her tone that made his stomach sink. He'd known that his brother wasn't a good husband, and he'd seen the sparkle in her eyes slowly fade away over the span of their marriage. He'd tried to fix things as best he could. He'd lectured his brother a few times about how he treated his wife and took her for granted. He'd really tried! Had her life really been that terrible with Elijah that she wouldn't want another marriage?

If she'd said she just couldn't replace Elijah, he might feel better. But that wasn't what she meant, and he knew it.

A creaking noise came from that apple tree branch outside the window, accompanied by the *pop-pop-pop* of breaking wood, which made his heart freeze in his chest. Miriam seemed to be moving in slow motion, because she turned toward the window with an uncertain look on her face. Zaac leaped forward in the same moment and grabbed Miriam's arm before the branch exploded through the window with a rush of cold, wet wind.

Zaac pulled her solidly against him, using the side of his body to shield her and the baby from the wind and glass. It had been an instinctive movement, and he was glad, because when he looked down at Miriam's white face, and tiny Ivy as she sucked in a breath to wail, they both seemed to be in one piece. But something stung on his arm, and he looked down to see a shard a glass stuck in his skin, blood seeping into his shirt and spreading in crimson fingers.

"Ouch," he murmured, and without thinking, he reached down and grabbed the glass shard firmly and pulled.

"Don't do that!" Elmer and Miriam said at once.

But it was too late—the shard was out, and he put it down on the counter. The wound was bleeding a whole lot more, though. He picked up some cut white cloth from the counter and blotted it against his arm.

"Are you okay?" he asked Miriam. Ivy was crying, and Miriam bounced gently back and forth, rocking the baby for comfort.

"Are *you*?" Miriam shot back, and she reached over and put her hand firmly over the white cloth, pressing down hard. "That needs pressure. Lots of it."

"I'll deal with this after we get that window boarded up," Zaac replied.

Obie came into the room then, a basket held in front of him and his face almost as white as his beard.

"What happened?" the old man asked, his slippers crunching over glass as he went closer to look at the broken window. He seemed to piece it all together in a flash. "That tree has been nothing but trouble! The roots have been messing with the plumbing. I am going to chop that tree down! I will!"

Elmer silently picked up one of the strips of cut cloth, and as Miriam let go, he tied it around Zaac's arm firmly and knotted it. Zaac nodded his thanks to Elmer and looked around the kitchen. Glass glinted across the floor in dangerous shards, and half a tree branch hung across the kitchen sink.

"Just hold Ivy," Zaac said, zeroing back in on Miriam and the baby. "You hear me? As long as Ivy is in your arms, she's safe. Let's get you over to the stove, and stay there."

Miriam nodded, and Zaac looked around the kitchen once more as wind and rain whipped inside.

"Is there any wood, Obie?" he asked. "Something to board up that window?"

"There's some plywood in the basement," Obie replied. "I'll show you."

"Let's get our boots on," Zaac said. "Until we get this glass swept up, at least."

There was a job ahead of him, and that made Zaac feel better. Something to accomplish. Something to fix. The Englishers might even say something to conquer, but Amish men would never admit to that feeling. Fixing was sufficient for them.

But the most important thing was keeping Miriam and Ivy safe, and with that wet, cold wind rushing in the window, they needed to get that jagged hole in the window covered.

Priorities.

Miriam stood by the stove, the heat pumping comfortably against her. She adjusted the blanket to cover Ivy a little better, and then she felt a warm shawl settle around her shoulders. She looked up in surprise to see it was Zaac who'd brought it. He tugged at the front of the shawl to make sure it settled over her arms and over the baby, too; then he dropped to one knee, opened the stove door and pushed in another stick of wood.

He shut the door with a clang, then rose to his feet, and she felt his hand linger for a moment on her back before he wordlessly marched away again—wearing his boots now—following her grandfather down the basement stairs.

Miriam let out a wavering breath, her gaze locked on the empty doorway where he'd disappeared. That had been an oddly tender gesture to get her a shawl like that, and to put more wood in the stove, and her stomach gave a flutter, matching the leaves from the broken branch that lay across her kitchen sink, ruffling in the gusting wind.

Ankel Elmer picked up the limb and tossed it back outside. That was a start. Then he grabbed a broom from the corner and started to sweep, the curtains snapping in the rain-laden wind. Downstairs, she could hear some thumping and the deep murmuring voices of her grandfather and Zaac.

Zaac emerged first with a piece of plywood under one arm. Dawdie came up behind him carrying his black metal toolbox. The kitchen was getting very dim, the lights having blown out in the gusting wind, but they wouldn't be able to light the kerosene lamps until the window was boarded up.

Dawdie put his toolbox on the counter and pulled out a flashlight and a hammer. Elmer abandoned the broom then, and between the two of them, Zaac and Elmer got the sheet of plywood into place and started hammering nails to keep it secured. Zaac hopped up onto the counter and knelt there while he pounded in a nail. The room immediately felt warmer, and Ivy started to squirm again, turning her little searching mouth toward Miriam's neck.

"You're hungry again, are you?" Miriam asked.

With two more nails, Zaac hopped back down again, and Miriam moved over to the sink. The wind whistled softly where it wriggled past the plywood, but for the most part it was held at bay.

"Here…" Zaac opened the tin of formula and measured out one small scoop into the bottle, then filled it to the water line, screwed on the nipple and handed it back. His fingers brushed against hers, and for just a moment, their eyes met.

"Can you feed her while I start supper?" she asked.

Zaac nodded, and she eased the baby into his arms, and she felt a little tug of yearning as she let the baby go.

Miriam set about looking through cupboards and pulling out ingredients, Miriam couldn't help but recall that overheard conversation. Zaac was getting along with Elmer rather well—a good thing, at face value—but she had to wonder just how helpful Elmer was going to be in helping Zaac leave.

And how long had Zaac been feeling this way—longing for another life away from the Amish faith? How long had he been planning?

Because he could be sweet when he wanted to be—she looked over at Zaac feeding the baby—but he was also capable of hiding an awful lot. Zaac was likable, but he wasn't trustworthy. She'd have to remember that.

Later on that evening, after dinner and several hands of Dutch Blitz, Elmer went with his father upstairs to look at some old papers that Obie had held on to. Their voices murmured wordlessly through the floorboards, and Zaac and Miriam sat in chairs pulled up close to the stove.

This was the first time Zaac had been alone with Miriam since working together at the chocolate shop, and he found himself feeling a little bashful. At Black Bonnet, she'd been busy in the kitchen and he'd been serving customers. He'd tried making some simple conversation with her while they worked together, but she'd been reluctant. She didn't seem to like him, and he knew why.

Even back when Miriam and Elijah were first getting to know each other, she'd only had eyes for Elijah. Zaac had been there, too, and she'd never given him a second look. But disinterest had turned into something more active when he'd tried to speak up about the marriage—she didn't like him, and he could feel it.

Somehow, as he looked over at her in the soft kerosene light, seeing the baby in her arms and her head leaned back against the back of the rocking chair, the moment felt domestically snug. And domesticity had never been his right with her—that had been a pleasure that belonged to Elijah. Zaac had felt more for Miriam than he'd ever had a right to, but that didn't mean he was foolish enough to act on it.

He looked away quickly.

Maybe this tender wash of emotion was just because Miriam looked tired. Or because he'd be sleeping under this roof tonight. Ivy heaved a deep sigh in her sleep and curled her little fingers into a fist.

"Miriam—" he started, before she interrupted him.

"I overheard you talking with Elmer about leaving the faith," Miriam said quietly. Her voice was low enough that no one but he should hear her, and he was grateful for that. Zaac looked over nervously. He didn't realize anyone had overheard that conversation.

"Oh… Well…" What was he supposed to say? He couldn't deny it.

"You don't owe me explanations," she said.

"I haven't told anyone my plans yet," he said.

"You told Elmer."

"I mean, I haven't told anyone at home—anyone who'd care either way."

Miriam looked over at him, her dark eyes filled with swimming emotion. Did that mean she would care if he left?

"With Elijah gone, if you leave the community, it will kill your mother," Miriam said.

So she was worried about his *mamm*. Very noble of her,

but it would have been nice to know that him leaving the community would affect her in some small way.

"I'll come back and visit," he said.

"I thought you were the reliable one," she said.

"I am."

"Not really. You're jumping the fence. Elijah might have been a rebel, but he wasn't leaving the community, was he?"

He didn't like the comparison with his brother. Elijah had been incredibly difficult to deal with, and Zaac had done his best to keep his brother under control. Miriam had no idea.

"This isn't about Elijah," he said. "This is about me, and I've been thinking on it for a while."

"So why are you leaving, then?" There was a tightness in her voice—she cared, it seemed.

"Because we have a beautiful life here, but we don't share it," he replied. That was the simple answer, but he knew no one else understood this or why it mattered to him.

"What do you mean?" Miriam squinted at him. "We're a community. We share everything!"

"I mean we don't welcome others into our community," he said quietly. "We don't share this life with outsiders."

She gave him a surprised look. *Yah*, that was the reaction he got when he tried bringing the topic up with some other men—they didn't understand him. But he wanted Miriam to understand this. Someone should.

"Look, we use our language and our unique way of life to keep Englishers out. *Yah*, we let them come see us as tourists, but we don't let them come in much closer. And we certainly don't seek them out to try and bring them into our way of life."

"Of course not!" Miriam exclaimed.

"And that's my problem. I think we're wrong, Miriam.

We should be bringing people in. We should be sharing our way of life and our hope with others."

"There is the problem of influence," she said, and he saw a spark in her eyes. This was touching a nerve for her. "Elijah didn't learn his drinking from us, did he? Or his gambling. And he was out drinking at an Englisher bar."

"*Yah*, and I see the problem…" Zaac sighed. It wasn't that he disagreed with everything in their Amish faith. He saw the logic and the reason. He saw why they lived a particular life that kept them close to home and close to each other. "But I can't get past the fact that Jesus told us to go out there and spread the good news, and we don't do that."

"And that's why you want to leave?" she asked.

He paused. It was the reason he was willing to share. There was more to it, of course. There was the fact that he'd been in love with his brother's wife, and the guilt that brought. He needed space—a lot of space—to get his balance back again. Because seeing her at church every other Sunday and seeing her in Aent Esther Mae's shop, or simply seeing her around the community, was getting more and more painful. He deserved that pain; he should have found a way to see her as a sister only, but he hadn't been able to.

"*Yah.* That's why," he said.

Miriam cast him a wry smile. "That's too bad."

"Why?" he asked.

"Because it would be easier to argue with something else," she replied, and she met his gaze, making his heart skip a beat at her directness.

Zaac chuckled and turned his attention back to the stove. "*Danke.*"

"For what?"

"For seeing that I've got a point."

Would he tell her the full reason of why he was leaving

before he left? Tonight, he thought he might, but in the light of day, he'd probably change his mind. His feelings for her were his own burden to bear, and he didn't need to dump it on her, too.

"Is there another reason why you're going?" she asked.

Zaac froze. "What do you mean?"

"Is there a girlfriend?" she asked. "Someone you'll marry?"

Zaac felt a rush of relief. "No," he said with a low laugh. "No, nothing like that. I want to do the right thing by my conscience. That's all."

"That's why Ankel Elmer left, you know," she said. "For Aent Trish."

"That's not why I'm leaving," he said, sobering. "There is no woman luring me away. This is about me."

Overhead, he could hear the squeaking floorboards of someone walking upstairs. Miriam smothered a yawn behind the back of one hand. She was tired. So was he, but more than that, she was starting to dig into his reasons, and if she got too close to the truth, he was afraid he might just say it. And that was something he would definitely regret in the light of day.

"You look tired," Zaac said. "Why don't I sleep down here by the stove?"

"No! I couldn't let a guest sleep in the kitchen, Zaac. Ankel Elmer is in a single bed, and Dawdie has a double. So maybe…"

"He isn't feeling well and he needs his rest," Zaac said. "And your bedroom is yours, obviously. But here's what I'm thinking. You were planning on having Ivy sleep in the basket, right?"

"*Yah*. That would be safest for her."

"It might also be a little bit chilly upstairs," he pointed

out. "I can stay down here and keep the stove burning overnight. I'll sleep on the floor if you've got a camping mattress or something I can use, and I can watch Ivy. When she wakes up, I'll get her a bottle. It should be simple enough. And I'll keep the kitchen warm so that she doesn't get chilled."

Miriam frowned slightly. "You'd be willing to do that?"

"Of course," he replied. "If you're worried about Ivy, I can promise to tap on your door if I need any help with her. I won't be a hero."

Miriam compressed her lips at his turn of phrase. It was decidedly English, but it made the point, too.

"That would be very kind of you," Miriam said, and pulled the basket toward her with her foot and leaned forward to ease the baby off her body. Then she lowered her into the blanket-lined basket. She held her hand between the baby and the stove, testing the heat.

Zaac held his hand next to hers, then scooched the basket back about a foot. Miriam tested the air, then nodded, too.

"That seems about right," she said. "She might get fussy."

"Then I'll hold her," he said. "I do know how to hold a baby."

"Support her head," Miriam said anyway.

He nodded. "I will."

Then Miriam stood up. "We have a bed roll in the storage room. I'll go get it for you, and some blankets."

"Danke," Zaac said, and as she walked briskly from the room, he squatted next to the sleeping baby.

No, there was no other woman who had a claim to his heart. If there was, he might feel less guilt. Elijah had been lured off the narrow path with parties and drinking, and Zaac couldn't help but feel like he hadn't done enough to help his brother become the husband he should've been.

Instead, Zaac had been angry. And he'd been thinking that if he'd married Miriam, she wouldn't have had to deal with the unique kind of misery that Elijah had brought home to her. That had been wrong. Maybe if Zaac had tried harder with his brother instead of harboring jealousy, he might have made a difference and Elijah might be alive today... and Miriam's baby might be, too.

So Zaac felt like he needed to go out and find people who needed help, because he needed to atone for his own mistakes. Gott had told his people to go out into all the world, and Zaac would do just that.

Gott forgive me...

It was a prayer he prayed often. But so far, he didn't feel forgiven.

Chapter Four

That night, Miriam lay in her bed feeling weary but unable to sleep. She'd left Zaac with bedding and plenty of wood, and now, lying under her quilt, she couldn't help but listen to the quiet sounds of him settling in for sleep. She heard the stove door open and clang shut again. Some rustling around, then silence. A moment later, a little more rustling, then silence again.

Her arms felt empty, and a hot tear trickled down her cheek. Somehow holding Ivy had felt different from holding a niece or a nephew. Those children had mothers whom she knew well. This tiny baby was without a mother, and she was without her child, and somehow they'd come together like two puzzle pieces. She was still grieving, and Ivy must be grieving, too, although she couldn't express it. The mother Ivy knew was gone, and somehow, she seemed to know that Miriam would stand in her place.

It was best to leave the baby with Zaac downstairs. It was best. She wiped the tears from her face. Zaac would care for her, and Miriam would be wise not to get overly attached to little Ivy. But Ivy wasn't the only one who would leave. Zaac was planning his escape, too, and that had stunned her. Somehow, even with her hard feelings for him, Zaac had felt like a pillar around here—a man who'd always be resolutely Amish—and his decision to leave had shaken her more than she wanted him to know.

Lying there in the quiet, listening to the soft pinging of the stovepipe below, she remembered Zaac as she'd known him over the years. He'd been a year ahead of her and Elijah in school, and he hadn't hung out with them much. Then he'd started his Rumspringa, and she'd been watching the older *kinner*, wondering what they'd do with their new-found freedom. Zaac had been cautious and quiet. *Boring.* That was what she'd thought of him back then. He hadn't taken risks. He hadn't broken any rules. Now she saw how immature she'd been to think a reserved, reliable man was boring. Because Elijah was anything but, and their marriage had been exhausting. What she wouldn't have given for a little boring predictability from Elijah!

Zaac had talked to her a few times back then, so she'd felt like she'd known him, but apparently not. Because when she and Elijah started courting, Zaac had been solidly against it. And that still hurt! What had been so terrible about her that he'd thought his brother would be better off with another girl?

Miriam slipped into a fitful sleep until she awoke to the sound of the baby's thin cry filtering up from the kitchen below. It took her a moment to shake off the fog of sleep. It was still night; she could see nothing but blackness outside the window. The baby's cry came louder now, and the pane rattled with the slap of wind and rain. The room wasn't too cold with the stovepipe coming through, but it wasn't exactly warm, either. She pushed back her covers with a shiver, wondering if Zaac would even wake up. Tired men could sleep like logs—she knew this from growing up with brothers and cousins. But then she heard the low rumble of Zaac's voice. She couldn't make out words, just the soft, reassuring tone, nearly drowned out by the howling wind and thrashing rain outside her window.

Miriam pulled on a robe and cinched it around her waist. Then she opened her bedroom door with a soft creak and slipped out of her room. The hallway was chilly upstairs, but when she got to the staircase, the warmth from the kitchen stove met her toes. She sank down to sit on the stairs, watching as Zaac gently patted Ivy's back, talking quietly to her as he headed over to the counter in the dim kitchen light. He was fully dressed—he must have slept that way.

"You're hungry, are you?" Zaac was saying as Ivy let out her little complaining cries. "I understand. You need your formula. No worries. I'll get it…"

Miriam had left a bottle with some powdered formula in the bottom, and he filled that, screwed on the nipple and shook it up. He turned then, and his gaze landed on her. Zaac gave her a rueful smile.

"Sorry, I wasn't quiet enough?"

"I woke up when she cried," Miriam said, and rose from the stair and went to light the kerosene lamp. She blinked in the sudden brightness as the kitchen blazed into a warm glow. "You look like you're used to this."

"I've been around babies," Zaac said. "I've seen it done."

He put the bottle down and adjusted Ivy in his arms, but getting her into the right position seemed to be more of a challenge, especially with Ivy squirming and turning her head toward him hungrily, as newborns did.

"Here," Miriam said. "I'll help you."

Zaac started to hand the baby over to her, but she shook her head. She'd been dreaming she was pregnant again, and that always left her emotions a little raw. Not tonight. There was something particularly bonding about the darkest hours and a hungry babe. She pushed back the urge to pull Ivy into her own arms.

"No, no," Miriam said. "You'll feed her. Just hold her like this."

She adjusted Ivy so that he could get a grip on one of her little legs, and she guided the bottle into the baby's searching mouth. Ivy connected with the bottle with a powerful slurp.

"She's getting stronger, isn't she?" Zaac murmured.

"Yah..." The baby did seem to be doing much better than when they'd first found her that evening. A few bottles of formula and some warmth by the fire seemed to be doing well by her.

Ivy opened and shut her little hands as she drank and pushed out a leg in enthusiasm. Miriam ran a hand over that thin little leg. Her skin was so soft, and she was so tiny and helpless...

"Zaac, there's something I wanted to say to you," Miriam said slowly. "It's something that was hard to say in front of other people."

Zaac looked over at her. She noticed a faint shadow of stubble on his chin. "What's that?"

"I was not a bad wife," she said, her voice low.

He was silent, and he pressed his lips together into a thin line, his attention back on the baby. His hair was mussed up, flattened on one side. It was a little endearing. He reminded her of her brothers when they used to stumble down for morning chores.

"I didn't say you were."

Not to her face, he didn't. But he'd said something to Elijah before the wedding, hadn't he? And then Elijah had gone absolutely wild once they were married. He hadn't settled down at all—and she'd truly believed he would!

"Some people thought I was a bad wife," she said. "Or that I must have been. They said that Elijah wouldn't have been out drinking and gambling if he'd had a warm and loving wife at home."

Zaac scowled. "Who said that?"

"People." She'd overheard some unmarried girls her age talking behind her back. There had been a fair dose of jealousy in the conversation, and she'd been reminded of the proverb about not listening to everything people say or you might hear them cursing you behind your back. That was what had happened. Had the girls really meant it? She hoped not, but the words had stung.

"I didn't hear anyone say that," he said. "If it makes you feel any better."

"Okay. Well, all the same, I was a good wife. I didn't nag Elijah—and maybe he could have used a little nagging, but I didn't. I always had a hot breakfast waiting for him and a hot dinner. I made his pack lunch for work. I had a smile on my face when he got home."

A pained look crossed Zaac's face, and she didn't know what it meant. Did he not believe her?

"If your mother ever mentions it," Miriam said, "you could tell her the truth. I was a good wife to Elijah. He didn't have any excuse to act the way he did."

"Miriam, even if you'd nagged him like a blue jay, he wouldn't have had any good excuse to go drinking and racing like that," Zaac said. "His death wasn't your fault."

Those words flooded her with unexpected relief, and tears prickled at her eyes.

"Danke."

"Are you okay?" he asked.

Miriam forced herself to meet his stare. Ivy finished the bottle then, and Zaac put it down on the table.

"I'm fine. Let me burp her," Miriam said.

Zaac handed her the baby, his warm arm pressing momentarily against her side as they exchanged the infant. She settled the baby on her shoulder, and Ivy pulled her knees up into a scrunchy little ball. Miriam rubbed her back and patted gently. It was a strange relief to get this little one back into her own arms. The warm weight of the baby against her chest was like a poultice against her own pain.

"Look, I knew my brother really well," Zaac said. "And he just had this rebellious streak in him. If he felt like someone was trying to control him, he'd push against it. And a wife has a few expectations. Of course she does. There is nothing wrong with that. Elijah was just the kind of man who was always trying to prove that he was independent."

"*Yah*, that's true," she murmured.

"He didn't listen to you," Zaac said.

"No, not at all," she replied. "Not for the big things. Not when it really mattered."

Zaac nodded. "He didn't listen to me, either."

And she was reminded again of that little talk Zaac had had with Elijah after their engagement, when he'd told Elijah he shouldn't marry her. Zaac had been trying to control them then, and Elijah had been furious. It had driven Elijah right into her arms.

Ivy burped, and when Miriam looked down at her, those little eyes were closing groggily. She was ready to be put back to bed.

Miriam went over to the basket next to Zaac's rumpled blankets and laid Ivy back down. Zaac put his body between the baby and the stove, and he opened the door and pushed in another couple sticks of wood. He used the poker to arrange the wood and then closed it again. But he remained with his back to them for another couple of beats.

There had been a time when the bishop had come to visit Elijah. She'd stood in the other room, listening while the bishop told him that he was behaving badly and needed to stop the drinking and gambling. He told him he had a responsibility to his wife and his future *kinner*. He told him that if he loved her, he'd smarten up. It was everything that Miriam had wanted to say but couldn't say so directly, and she'd been deeply grateful that the bishop had spoken to her husband man-to-man.

But Elijah had been furious with her after the bishop had a prayer with them as a couple and then left. Elijah hadn't spoken to her for days after that. He'd frozen her out, and he'd stayed away for two days. He thought that she had reported him, but Miriam hadn't.

And somehow she'd thought Elijah had probably told his family about it and made her look bad. It was good to know that he hadn't.

"Are you serious about not marrying again?" Zaac asked.

"Yah." She crossed her arms over her chest, guarding against the chill closer to the stairs.

"You really don't want a family?"

She did want a family—very much—but she didn't trust that it would work out the way her parents' marriage had anymore. She'd thought all husbands were considerate, kind and devoted to their wives. She'd been wrong there.

"I want something I can count on," she said. "Your *aent* has a life that no one can take away from her. She's worked hard, and she's built up a business that makes a difference in people's lives. She's beloved, in our community and with the Englishers, too. And she has fun—she loves candymaking. The smile on her face when she gets to the shop is not reliant on a man's mood that morning. If she works hard, she sees the results."

"And Elijah gambled everything away."

"I was making coffee soup with leftover heels of bread," she said. "I was scraping the root hairs off wilted carrots to make our dinner. I will never be reliant on a man to make sure I can eat again, Zaac. Never."

Zaac dropped his gaze, his expression sober. "I get it. And I'm so sorry. If I'd known you didn't have groceries, I would have brought food for you."

"It was my husband's place to use his paycheck on our necessities."

"Still."

It would have only made Elijah angry if people came by with charity. He was happier having her hide the truth than accepting help from his family and having them know the worst.

She angled her head to the side in acceptance. "*Danke.* It's a kind thought, but I didn't say anything to anyone. Even when the bishop came to visit and reprimanded Elijah, it wasn't because I'd told anyone anything. That wasn't me."

"I believe you," he said.

Did he truly believe her? Because the young unmarried women had turned against her then. They thought she'd been disloyal to her husband—a man they'd found rather handsome and charming. Maybe they thought they could have made him happier. It didn't matter now.

"Marriage was very hard," she admitted. "It was painful. I cried a lot. When I think about getting married again, I'm filled with dread. I know that people will judge me for that."

"We can't argue with each other's very good reasons for making unpopular choices. I think we almost count as friends."

"Is that friendship?" she asked with a soft laugh.

"*Yah*, I'd say so." His eyes warmed.

Somehow, that thought softened her just a little bit. Were they becoming friends after all this time? Maybe so—just in time to bid each other farewell and turn to their own goals.

"Good night, Zaac."

"Good night," he replied.

The kerosene lamp went out as she made her way up the steps, and as she got to the top, she heard the sound of Zaac getting back under his covers.

The wind howled, and the rain drummed down on the roof and thrashed against the windows. But all the same, she felt better. Her decision to build a life like Esther Mae's wouldn't be supported by the community at large. They'd want her to marry again, to put her heart into another man and have *kinner*. She knew that, and that was why she'd decided to simply go about building that life and tell no one about her plans. But having Zaac, of all people, understand her was a comfort, too. Just being understood made her feel a little more confident.

She could do this.

Zaac awoke the next morning at his usual hour of four thirty, and the baby was just starting to fuss and stir herself awake. It had taken some time to fall asleep again last night after he and Miriam had fed the baby. She wasn't planning on marrying again, and that made sense. Elijah had been a terrible husband, but Zaac hadn't known that Miriam had been struggling to keep food on their table.

They wouldn't have starved, but the humiliation of having to go to others for food would have been a terrible thing. Sometimes a man could forget that women had to put their entire lives in their hands. Paying bills, buying food, keeping themselves in decent dresses—that was all dependent on her husband's ability to provide. He could only imagine how unsettling it would be to watch the wage earner of the home squandering the small income he made.

So he did understand her desire to stay single. If she had a way to provide for herself, she'd at least know that her bills could be paid. After having her trust broken on such a fundamental level, trusting a man again would be difficult. And that was sad because she'd been a good wife.

Zaac had tried to talk to his brother about his behavior, but Elijah had said everything was fine and they loved each other. Except, when a man loved a woman well, he didn't leave her thin, sad and exhausted. When the bishop had taken Elijah aside and spoken to him about his behavior, it wasn't because Miriam had reported him—it was because Zaac had.

Footsteps on the staircase drew his gaze as he folded up his blankets, and Miriam came downstairs fully dressed.

"She slept through the rest of the night?" she asked as she bent down over the basket. She hesitated a moment and then gathered the baby up in her arms. "Did you finally get a full tummy, sweetheart?"

Her gaze softened and her voice lowered when she talked to the baby, and his heart skipped a whole beat as he held his breath. All of her seemed to soften and almost shine as she looked down into the little face, and he watched Ivy's expression as her gaze locked onto Miriam's face and the baby completely stilled.

Yah, he felt it, too. There was something very soothing about Miriam, and when her attention was focused on a person, he didn't know how anyone kept a straight thought in their heads. She was…beautiful.

Zaac dropped his gaze, suddenly embarrassed. He headed over to the counter and measured out another bottle of formula for the infant. As he stirred it up, Miriam changed the baby's diaper, talking softly to her the whole time. This baby was doing better since they'd found her, and it wasn't just the formula that was making the difference. It was Miriam. There was something healing about her, and Elijah had missed it. As terrible as it was to think ill of the dead, he had to be honest, didn't he?

Elmer came downstairs next in his blue jeans and a flannel shirt, and Zaac gave him a nod.

"Morning," Elmer said.

Overhead, Zaac could hear Obie's footsteps moving around. The day had begun for sure and certain, and there were chores to do outside with the horses in the stable and the cattle out in the barn. Animals still needed care whether it was storming or not.

"I'm going to head out for chores just as soon as I wash up," Zaac said.

"I'll help you," Elmer said. "Four hands make for lighter work."

Zaac shot the older rancher a grin. For having jumped the fence, Elmer was still awfully Amish in some ways.

Five minutes later, they were both stepping into rubber boots and pulling coats on as thunder boomed outside. Rain pattered down, and as Zaac headed outside, a blast of wind brought it right in into his face. Lightning lit up the predawn sky, and a moment later, more thunder crashed.

This storm was not moving on. Not yet, at least. Zaac squinted through the downpour and lifted his kerosene lantern higher as he plunged through the deluge.

When they got into the stable, Zaac was dripping wet, water having found its way down his neck and down his back. He shivered and shook off his hat.

"It's not letting up, is it?" Elmer asked as he pulled the door shut.

They hung the lantern on a hook, and the horses nickered a greeting.

"Doesn't seem to be," Zaac replied. He shook out his coat, headed to the first stall and grabbed the water bucket to refill. The tall black gelding snorted—he hadn't been expecting a stranger, obviously. "Elmer, can I ask you something?"

"Sure."

"We heard that you left the Amish for your wife," he said.

Elmer shrugged. "I mean, partly. I had been thinking about it for a long while, and when I fell in love with Trish, that sped things up for me."

So that rumor had been right. Zaac didn't have anyone out there waiting on him. When he left the Amish, he would be doing it utterly alone.

"Marrying *the right* Englisher made things easier," Elmer said with a chuckle. "Trish is my Eve. She's the one Gott made for me. So everything is easier with her at my side. But *yah*, having an Englisher wife does make things easier. She's taught me an awful lot."

For the first time, Zaac wondered who he was going to marry when he left the faith. Not an Amish girl, that was for sure and certain. Except that when he imagined a wife of his own, he was seeing a white *kapp*, a cape dress and bright eyes that lit up a whole room when she looked down at the baby in her arms...

His feelings for Miriam had been the problem all along. Loving a woman had paved the way for Elmer to leave. For Zaac, loving Miriam was going to be what chased him out.

They added hay to the feeders, and some grain as a

treat for the horses, as the lightning cracked overhead and the wind howled. Mucking out the stalls didn't take too long. They were finished and taking the wheelbarrow of soiled hay outside to dump when Elmer suddenly stopped.

"What's that?" Elmer asked, listening.

"What's what?" Zaac looked over his shoulder, but then the wind and rain hit his face and he ducked his head against the onslaught. He pushed the wheelbarrow as quickly as he could toward the muck pile behind the stable. He tipped the contents onto the pile and turned back just as Elmer came out of the stable, hunched over something in his hands. He closed the door behind him and pointed toward the house.

"I found a kitten!" Elmer hollered through the crashing storm.

"What?"

"A kitten! Come on!"

Zaac jogged after Elmer back toward the house, and after they plunged back into the mudroom and pushed the door shut against another gust of wind, Elmer opened his hands to reveal a sodden little pile of fur in his palm.

"Where did you find it?" Zaac asked.

"Just by the door," Elmer said. "I looked around, and I couldn't find any more. Just the one."

Was it alive? Zaac looked closer, and then it moved, opening big liquid eyes and letting out a soft, pleading mew.

"I can't believe you heard it," Zaac said. "That kitten wouldn't have survived out there much longer."

The kitten stretched toward Zaac, and he caught it as it just about tumbled out of Elmer's hands.

"She wants you, it seems," Elmer said.

The kitten was as light as a bird, and it trembled in Zaac's hand, a wet, chilled little thing. Looking down at it, Zaac couldn't help but pity her. Such a difficult start in life, and so very small.

"Let's warm her up first," Zaac said. "Then we can head out to the barn and do the chores out there."

As they came into the warm kitchen, he spotted Miriam with the baby in her arms, rocking back and forth. She looked up in surprise, and her gaze fell down to Zaac's hands.

"What do you have there?" she asked.

Zaac held the kitten up. "A kitten." He winced. "I'm sorry. We just found another baby in need of warmth and milk."

Chapter Five

"Oh my!"

The kitten was so wet that Miriam hadn't been sure if it was indeed a kitten or a mouse! But when she looked closer, she saw that tiny pink nose and split muzzle, and a wee pink tongue when it opened its mouth in a mew. "Where are the others?"

Miriam leaned her cheek against Ivy's downy head as she looked toward the window. Another flash of lightning lit up the sky. Dawn had broken into a stormy, hazy gray, and she couldn't see the stable from here—not through the downpour.

"We have no idea," Ankel Elmer interjected. "I couldn't find them. I heard that one cry, and I found it just outside the door in a puddle. The poor thing must have fallen there somehow. I went back to look around, but I couldn't find the litter. It was just that one half-drowned kitten."

"At least there's only one," Miriam said. "Small mercies, I suppose."

They didn't have any cats here—not officially. But strays would find their way into the barn and stable, and they'd put out cat kibble to feed them in the winter when mousing was thin. It looked like a cat had had some kittens, and she could only hope the rest of the litter was with the mother somewhere dry and safe.

She came closer to look down at the poor little thing, and she adjusted Ivy in her arms. Ivy's little stomach was full of formula right now, and she dozed comfortably. Zaac's bandage poked out from under his shirtsleeve, and she touched it gingerly.

"How is your arm?" she asked.

"It'll heal."

That wasn't really an answer, but he didn't look like he'd give more than that, and she couldn't see more for herself.

"How's Ivy?" Zaac asked after a beat of silence.

"She's doing rather well." Miriam looked up at him, and they shared a satisfied little smile. They might have been at odds when it came to Elijah, but with Ivy, they felt like partners. They'd found her together, and somehow this infant felt like a shared success—hers and Zaac's. "I don't know if I'm imagining it, but I think she's just a little bit heavier than she was last night."

"I noticed that, too," Zaac said with a nod. "I think she grew."

"That fast?" she asked.

"We fed her well." He shrugged, but he shot a smile all the same. "We'll have to do the same for the kitten."

Dawdie's footsteps sounded on the staircase, and Miriam turned to see her grandfather descend, a handkerchief in one hand. He was fully dressed, one shirttail poking out of the waist of his pants. Miriam hadn't found a polite way to let her grandfather know about these little missed details, and so she did as she always did and pretended not to see it.

Dawdie's eyes looked watery and red, and he dabbed

at his nose and sniffled. Miriam's heart sank. Dawdie still wasn't feeling well. A simple cold could be hard on the old man at his age, but he was too stubborn to admit when he was sick until he was really ill. And that wasn't wise.

Ivy squirmed in Miriam's arms, and she looked down at the baby with a wave of aching tenderness. She couldn't let little Ivy catch a cold, either. Infants and the elderly were most vulnerable to these things, so she couldn't just hand the baby to Dawdie, which would have been her solution to getting breakfast started.

Zaac carried the tiny kitten to the stove to warm up, and he stood there, looking about as drenched as the little creature did. His hair was damp, and a drip of water hung from the bottom of his chin. His gaze flicked up and met hers, and he wiped the drip of water off his chin at the same time with a rueful little smile. Miriam's cheeks warmed. Something between them had changed since last night, and she found herself feeling a little bashful.

But she wasn't about to make a fool of herself, either. This time locked in together was complicated enough. She turned back to her grandfather.

"Dawdie, pull up a chair by the stove," Miriam said. "It's nice and warm there."

Ankel Elmer grabbed the chair just as Miriam spoke, and he settled it nice and close to the stove. Dawdie sank into it, dabbing at his nose again.

"Danke, sohn," Dawdie said. "Good morning, by the way. I just need some ginger tea, and I'll be right as rain."

Ginger tea was their first stop when any of them got a cold. It helped with coughs, and adding in some honey would soothe Dawdie's throat, too.

"I have a pot of water on the stove already and some

coffee started," Miriam said. She pulled the basket across the counter and eased the infant off her shoulders and laid her back inside. Ivy wriggled and screwed up her face in displeasure before she started her hiccuping wail. Once Ivy had gotten into Miriam's arms this morning, she didn't want to be put down. Miriam couldn't blame her. Was she missing her mother? Was she afraid of being abandoned again? How much did this newborn baby even understand?

"It's okay, Ivy," Miriam said softly, jiggling the basket. "I'm here. I just need free hands, little one. I'm here. I'm here."

It was the only thing Miriam could think to say. Ivy was not alone. Ivy's cries didn't stop, though, and Elmer came over to the basket and silently scooped the baby up. He was still a bit wet from being outside, and Miriam hurriedly looked around for a blanket. When she found one, she tossed it over her *ankel*'s shoulder. Elmer put the baby on top of the blanket, and he patted her little back with one warm palm. He hummed softly, gently patting, and the infant settled and stopped crying. Miriam gave her *ankel* an impressed nod.

"You forget I've raised three of my own," Elmer said with a wink. "I know my way around a fussy baby."

And as if to fill the newfound silence, the kitten started to mew again. Before Miriam could start work on their breakfast, the kitten was in need of some food, too. She went to the icebox and pulled out a pitcher of cream from yesterday and poured some into a dish. She grabbed an egg from the mesh container on the counter and separated the round orange yolk out into a bowl, then added it to the cream. She pulled a Costco-size bottle of corn syrup out of the cupboard and added a tablespoon, then started to whisk the simple formula together into a smooth, frothy mix.

"I'm not sure this kitten is old enough to lap milk yet," Zaac said. "Do you have an eye dropper?"

"No, but I have a straw." This wasn't her first newborn kitten in need of extra milk. "I've got some kitten formula in the barn, too. I can go get it later."

"You'll stay here where it's warm and dry," Zaac shot back. "We're doing chores out there, anyway. We'll bring it back for you."

Miriam was tempted to be annoyed at his bossy tone, but the intent behind it softened her. He just wanted to keep her out of the storm, so she gave him a small smile.

"Okay, then. But don't forget." Miriam put a plastic straw into the milk solution and then put her thumb on top to hold the liquid inside. She brought it over to the tiny kitten and touched the open end of the straw with a bead of formula hanging out to the kitten's mouth. The kitten opened her mouth in a little mew and turned her head around, crying plaintively.

"Come on…" Miriam murmured, following the kitten's mouth with the straw and dripping sticky formula into Zaac's palm. She looked up at him and caught his dark gaze locked on her with a little smile on his lips.

"I'm trying," Miriam said, and this time, she managed to get a drop of formula into the kitten's mouth. She swallowed hungrily.

"She's got the idea," Zaac said.

A couple more drops made it into the kitten's mouth before she seemed to understand where the food was coming from, and she started to drink up the formula as it touched her tongue. That emptied the milk, and Zaac took the straw from Miriam, his warm fingers sliding over hers.

"I've got it," he said, his voice low, and his gentle gaze flickered to meet hers again.

Her heart stammered in her chest, and she quickly dropped her gaze. Zaac was handsome, and now was not a good time to notice that.

"I'll get breakfast started," Miriam said, and when she looked over her shoulder, Zaac's attention was back on the kitten, his lips pursed in concentration as he guided the straw to the kitten's searching mouth. It was like that one heart-stopping look hadn't happened, and she almost questioned it herself.

Miriam grabbed a mug from the cupboard and some ground ginger tea. The kettle was steaming on the stove, and she set about fixing her grandfather his tea with a generous tablespoon of golden honey stirred in.

"Dawdie, your tea is ready," Miriam said cheerfully, handing him the mug.

"Can I get you some tea, Ankel?" she asked, turning to Elmer. "I've got coffee almost done, too."

"I like coffee in the morning, but I'll get my own," he replied.

And as Miriam set about starting breakfast, her gaze kept moving back to the chocolate, butterscotch chips and potato chips on the far end of the counter. She didn't need to get caught up in a handsome man's eyes. What she needed was a step into her future. Today, she'd try those chocolate-dipped potato chips and see just how good they were.

Zaac got a good amount of milk into the kitten, and as the heat from the stove gently dried her fur, she fluffed out until she turned into a little brindle ball. She curled up in Zaac's palm, tucking her little nose into her milk-full belly, and fell asleep. He lifted her to his ear, and he could make out the soft snores.

Obie pushed himself to his feet and put his mug on the counter.

"Well," the old man said. "Time for chores."

Zaac shot Elmer a questioning look. This was his father, after all, but Obie did not look well. He was obviously sick—although he'd push through, that was clear. Miriam looked over her shoulder in mild alarm, too.

"You can all stop doing that," Obie said. "This is life. We get the job done, even when it's hard. Stop acting all shocked and scandalized because a farmer does his job. It's not that alarming."

"I owe you some help," Zaac said. "You've given me a place to stay during this storm, and I appreciate it. Let me at least do the rest of the morning chores for you."

Obie stroked his white beard and eyed the window. A tree in Zaac's line of sight was thrashing in the gale.

"I'm particular about the calves," Obie said, shaking his head.

"I'd be grateful if you allowed me to do this for you," Zaac said, lowering his voice for the old man's ears alone. "I know it's not convenient having me here right now, and I want to make that up to you. Give me your instructions for the calves, and I'll follow them. You have my word."

Obie eyed him for a moment.

"I don't want Miriam to remember me as the man who didn't do his part, Obie," Zaac added quietly. "Please."

Obie's gaze moved past him toward his granddaughter. He looked thoughtful for a moment and then nodded. "That, she would, too. You're not her favorite man, Isaac."

"I realize that."

He had a lot to make up for—both in not doing more to help his brother and in not being warmer to Miriam. He'd thought he'd been doing the right thing by standing back and hiding his feelings. And he still felt it was right—but it had left Miriam feeling judged. And he regretted that much.

"Okay. Fine. *Danke* for the help today, Isaac. Hand me the kitten. I'll keep her warm, then. Might as well do something useful."

Zaac handed the kitten over to Obie, who cradled the tiny creature in his calloused hands. And when Zaac glanced toward Miriam once more, she silently mouthed the word *"Danke."*

It was the very least he could do for this family right now. The very least. And he'd been utterly truthful with the old man. He did want Miriam to see better of him than she had up until now. But he also needed to occupy his time while Miriam was so close, and if that meant doing chores, then all the better. His heart was not safe this close to her.

"Now, for the little Holstein bull calf," Obie went on, "he needs a bottle and a half of milk. Mind, you need to give him that extra half, even if he doesn't seem inclined to drink it…"

After Obie had finished giving his instructions, Zaac and Elmer headed out through the driving rain toward the barn. It was a longer walk, and Zaac didn't even pretend he was going to stay dry. He simply accepted the rain down his collar and the wet in his boots, and trudged on.

He found the calves as Obie said he would, and he set about following the instructions he'd been given. Together, the men mucked out stalls and filled feeders and water troughs. And before they headed back, Zaac turned toward a bank of cupboards.

"Do you know where the kitten formula is?" Zaac asked Elmer.

The older man shook his head. "In those cupboards somewhere, I imagine."

So they started looking. There were bottles of bovine medication, some first aid supplies for both people and cattle. There were calf coats for newborn calves in cold weather, extra calf bottles, a package of mousetraps, some work gloves, an extra pair of rubber boots…and in the back of the third cupboard he opened, Zaac found a resealable plastic bag of kitten formula.

"Found it," he said, and Elmer shut the door of the cupboard he'd been searching.

"All right," Elmer said, and he looked toward the blowing storm outside. "I guess we'd better get back."

"Breakfast should be ready when we get in," Zaac said.

Elmer cast him a grin. "I appreciate what you did for my *daet* in there. He's stubborn when he's proving a point, and you just…managed him really well."

"I didn't mean to manage him," Zaac replied. "I just wanted to make sure I was the one stomping through the storm and not him."

"It amounts to the same thing," Elmer replied. "You put his safety first, and you made him feel like a man still. That can be delicate. Well done, is all I'm saying. Let's get back."

Zaac rolled the compliment over in his head as they plunged back through the storm. Did that mean Elmer thought he could manage a ranch? Perhaps that was too big of a stretch, but Zaac appreciated the older man's words all the same. Elmer didn't seem like a man who threw compliments around willy-nilly.

When they got back into the house again, Zaac was met with the warm, sweet scent of pancakes. He shook out his wet coat and hung it on a peg, then stepped out of the muddy work boots and left them on the mat. He'd be back into them soon enough. Then he and Elmer headed into the toasty kitchen. Ivy was fast asleep in her basket, the tip of her pink tongue sticking out of her mouth as she made little sucking movements in her sleep. And Obie was in a rocking chair now, the kitten on his knee.

"The calves?" Obie asked.

"*Yah*, I did as you told me to do," Zaac said. "And I've brought the kitten formula, too."

"All right, then…" Obie said, leaning back again.

Miriam stood at the stove next to them, flipping pancakes in a cast-iron pan. Zaac was wet and cold, so he stood next to her, letting the heat from the stove warm up his clothes. She smelled nice—like soap and baking— and he tried to keep his attention on his cold hands, not Miriam.

"Are you hungry?" Miriam asked.

"*Yah,*" Zaac said. "I'm famished."

"Good." Her smile flickered in his direction. "Because breakfast is almost ready. I just need to go downstairs and get some preserves."

"Let me take over with the pancakes," Elmer said.

Elmer took over at the stove, and Miriam headed down the basement stairs.

"Isaac, why don't you carry the jars for her?" Obie said. "They can be heavy."

Zaac swallowed. He'd been trying to avoid more time alone with her, but he couldn't very well refuse, either, so he nodded in silent acceptance and followed her down the narrow staircase. As he reached the bottom, Miriam picked up a kerosene lantern on a little shelf and struck a match to light it. Then she placed it on a hook that hung down from the ceiling. The light glowed softly on her face, casting soft shadows that made the cozy space feel even snugger. Above them, Elmer's and Obie's voices were muffled and distant. Miriam looked at him questioningly.

"Your *dawdie* asked me to carry the jars for you," he said.

"Oh… *Danke*."

Now he felt just a little bit foolish standing in the cellar with her, but he'd do his duty and help with the heavy lifting. Miriam started scanning the wooden shelves by the low kerosene light—ruby red cherries, crimson beets, golden pears, bright carrots and the foggy brine of dill pickles.

"There is something that has been bothering me," Miriam said, her back to him as she searched.

"What's that?" he asked.

She turned then. "You told your brother not to marry me."

Zaac's heart skipped a beat. What exactly had his brother told her? She met his gaze evenly, waiting for his response. He tried to swallow and failed.

"I…did talk to my brother about marrying you." He knew how bad this sounded, but he couldn't lie.

"Why?" She shook her head and turned away. "Why would you try and break us up? I was a good wife to him. You've said so yourself."

"You were."

"So what made me not good enough before the wedding?" she demanded.

"It wasn't you who wasn't good enough," Zaac said. "It was him."

Miriam blinked at him. "What?"

"I knew my brother," Zaac said. "He wasn't anything serious enough. He was still hanging out with some questionable people, and he was drinking more than he should. My *mamm* thought that marrying you would settle him down, and I—" He pressed his lips together, remembering his argument with his mother about this very thing. She'd been adamant that if he tried to stop his brother's blessings, Gott would not be able to bless Zaac.

And maybe she'd been right, because Zaac had stayed in this awful limbo ever since—feeling more for Miriam than he should and shouldering that constant guilt.

"I disagreed with her," Zaac concluded. "I saw my brother acting like his actions wouldn't hurt anyone, and then I saw you—"

She was beautiful—soft, expressive eyes, pink lips and a chin he longed to touch.

"What about me?" she asked cautiously.

"You were good and kind, and hardworking," Zaac said. "You believed in our way of life, and you loved Gott honestly. Miriam, you were too good for him."

"You expect me to believe that you warned him off me because I was too good?"

"I don't lie," he said quietly. "And I didn't warn him that you were too good. If you loved each other and wanted to be together, who was I to make that kind of judgment? I warned him that he'd make you miserable."

Miriam blinked. Her lips parted, but nothing came out. He'd told his brother that if he kept on this path, drinking and partying and dancing just a step away from being caught by the elders, a girl like Miriam would be humiliated. Zaac couldn't tell her that Elijah would be a devoted and loving husband when in reality he'd be an irresponsible one. Elijah had told him where to get off, and Zaac had left it alone. He'd tried.

"I think I was right about that," he added.

"I was not miserable!" she finally said.

"You sure looked deeply unhappy. You were losing weight, and you were pale all the time. The shine went out of your eyes, and out of your hair. You were always watching Elijah and jumping to make sure he was happy. That's not what a happy woman looks like. You looked incredibly stressed out all the time."

"I did?"

"Yah."

"Oh…"

"And my brother looked…just fine. He was perfectly happy, perfectly rested. Fresh as a daisy, while you were wasting away."

Miriam's expression faltered.

"I'm not insulting your looks, Miriam," he added. "You're a beautiful woman—you really are. But when a man loves a woman, he makes her life easier, not harder. He takes care of her, and listens to her, and builds a future with her that they both can enjoy. After a woman gets married, she normally puts on a little happy weight, and gets a special sparkle in her eye and some color in her cheeks. My sister did. My cousins did. I don't know what happened behind closed doors, but you looked like a woman who wasn't being loved properly."

Tears welled in Miriam's eyes, and she looked away. "I thought I needed to do better."

"Loving him should have been enough, Miriam! What else did he want from you?"

And right now, Zaac honestly wanted to know. What had Elijah been telling her? What ridiculous complaints was she silently carrying in her heart?

"I wish I knew," she said. "I constantly felt like I was failing."

His heart ached for her. She thought she was the one who was failing? That was Elijah! And Elijah should have been telling her daily what a great wife she was. That was *his* responsibility.

"You weren't failing. You deserved to be treated better than you were," he said.

She sucked in a wavering breath, and he could see her pulse fluttering at the base of her neck. She was so pretty, standing there among these jars of preserves— and that proved his point, didn't it? A woman could be standing in the basement next to plywood shelving, and she'd still make a man's heart skip a beat if he honestly cared about her.

"I thought I hid it," she whispered.

"Not from me," he said gruffly.

He'd been watching, and he'd been doing his best to keep an eye on Elijah, too, to make sure he behaved himself. It had been both heartbreaking to watch Miriam struggling and exhausting to try to keep up with Elijah's antics. Zaac knew what it meant when a woman looked miserable and the husband looked just fine. It meant there was a gross misbalance there, and the wife was being tilled under—whether the husband meant to or not. But Zaac had said enough. He didn't want to embarrass her, and maybe he didn't want to admit how closely he'd been watching, either.

"What jars should I bring upstairs?" he asked, his voice low.

"Cherries," she whispered.

They were above her head, so he reached past her and pulled down a jar.

"Two, please," she said.

He reached up again, and this time her gaze came up, and he found himself just a whisper away from her. He could see the faint freckles splashed across her cheeks, and when her lips parted, he found that he couldn't drag his eyes away from them. All he could think about was dipping his head down and catching those lips with his. His heart thundered in his ears. This was something he'd thought about too many times… It was almost muscle memory. But so was the guilt that came with it.

"Miriam?" Obie's voice came from the door at the top of the stairs, and Zaac shut his eyes, breaking the moment.

He opened them again and grabbed the second jar of cherries.

"Coming!" Miriam called, and her voice sounded a little strangled. *Yah*, he felt the same way.

She turned and picked up a jar of pink applesauce, but then she paused, her gaze flickering back up to meet his. He smiled ruefully, and a smile touched her lips in return; then she headed past him toward the stairs.

Zaac followed, a jar of cherries in each hand, and he tried to calm the pattering of his own heartbeat.

Miriam was a great cook and a skilled homemaker already, but that wasn't what drew him to her like a cold man drawn to a woodstove. Today, in the chilly cellar, it was as simple as the way she softened just a little bit when her gaze met his. It was in the defiant way she could raise one eyebrow and in the curve of her lips just before she smiled.

There was just something about Miriam. She could have been a terrible cook for all it mattered and he'd happily choke down whatever she put in front of him. But he didn't know how to put it into words, and that was probably for the best.

He wasn't staying, and she wasn't marrying again. They both knew exactly where this stood, and there was no future between them. Whatever he was feeling needed to stop here and now.

Chapter Six

⟨ornament⟩

Miriam hurried up the stairs with the applesauce clutched in front of her and her heart hammering in her throat. What had just happened? There had been a moment when Zaac's gaze had met hers, and her stomach had fluttered, and she'd seen how tenderly he looked down at her... She'd never been looked at quite like that before. Ever.

And Zaac had been paying attention. He'd noticed how hard things had been for her and how tired she'd been from trying to be enough for Elijah. No one else had seemed to notice—or at least, no one else had said anything.

Her grandfather waited at the top of the staircase, the kitten cupped against his chest, and she realized belatedly that she'd also wanted a jar of peaches from the cellar, but she'd been too flustered to remember, and she was not going back now. Zaac's sure footsteps came up behind her, and she shot her grandfather a smile. She could feel how close Zaac was, though, and some foolish part of her felt a little safer just for his presence.

"We have the fruit," she said to her grandfather, and she sounded just a little too cheery in her own ears.

Ivy started to fuss in her basket, and Miriam deposited the applesauce on the counter and headed over to the basket. She needed some relative privacy to settle her own feelings, and when she gathered the infant up against her chest, she felt her blood pressure lower. Ivy settled, too, and Miriam touched her cheek against the baby's silky hair.

Elmer had tied a towel around his waist with a length of bailing twine, and he flipped some pancakes in the greased pan with an expert flair. Her uncle did seem to know his way around a kitchen, and the pancakes smelled very good.

"Let's eat!" Elmer said cheerfully. "I don't know about all of you, but I'm starving."

After breakfast was finished, Elmer and Dawdie headed into the sitting room to read the *Budget* and catch up on the local news, leaving Miriam and Zaac alone. Ivy had fallen asleep again and lay in her basket near the stove.

"Would you do me a favor?" Miriam asked.

"Uh—*yah*. Of course."

"I'm going to make those dipped potato chips, and I want you to be my taste-tester."

"Twist my arm," he said with a low laugh.

"No, I'm serious, though. I want you to be completely honest. I'm not looking for politeness. I need you to tell me exactly what you think of them—an unbiased review, as it were."

"*Yah*, I can try," he said.

He liked the idea of taste-testing chocolate, he had to admit. He settled down at the table, watching her work; he had a feeling he'd only get in the way.

She set about melting chocolate, butterscotch chips and peanut butter chips in separate pots. She had water in each pot and a bowl on top to hold the melting candy. She worked quickly, and as the chocolate started to melt, she stirred each dish.

"Oh, those caramels in the box on the counter—those are something I thought up, too," she said. "Can you try one or two and tell me what you think?"

Zaac got up and went to the counter. He pried the lid off a Tupperware container and pulled out a soft, square caramel with a creamy swirl on top that looked like icing, but when he took a taste, he realized it wasn't. It was a sort of cashew cream—the sweetness of the caramel offsetting the cashew cream to perfection. He chewed slowly, and Miriam's gaze flickered toward him.

"Amazing," he said, sucking the caramel off his teeth.

Her expression stayed serious. "No, I don't want compliments. I want to know what you think. People aren't going to buy something like this just because they like my smiling face. It has to be tasty enough to sell—that's the bar."

"It's not what I expected," he said. "I thought it was icing on top, but it's not. I like the cashew flavor, and it goes really well with the caramel."

"Would you buy it?" she asked.

"*Yah*, definitely."

She nodded, satisfied, and turned back to the stove. Zaac popped another caramel into his mouth. Ivy started to fuss in her basket, and still chewing slowly, Zaac went over and picked her up. He put her up on his shoulder, adjusting her blanket to keep her covered snuggly.

Miriam brought the bowls to the table and set them on hot pads. Her gaze stopped at Ivy, and her expression softened in that way she had when she was around the newborn.

"All right, I'm going to try some different combinations," she said, and she opened the bag of chips. She selected a large, unbroken rippled potato chip. She dipped it in one dish, let the liquid drip off and then laid it on a plate. She took another chip and did the same in a different bowl. When the candy had hardened one chip, she dipped it again into a bowl of chocolate and then returned it to the plate to harden again.

She worked slowly, laying the chips in a straight line in different combinations.

The first one Zaac selected was white chocolate and butterscotch, and he chewed thoughtfully.

"Too sweet," he said.

Miriam grabbed a pad of paper and jotted down a note.

"Okay, try that one—peanut butter and chocolate."

Zaac did as she instructed and took a bite. The crunch and salt of the chip was the perfect contrast to the peanut butter and chocolate.

"Mmm. I like this one. Really good."

"And this one—dark chocolate and butterscotch?"

That one was better, the dark chocolate cutting the sweetness.

"What if we tried a chip dipped in just one?" Zaac said. "Just chocolate or just butterscotch?"

Miriam complied, dipping a chip in milk chocolate. She let the liquid chocolate drip back into the bowl, then laid it on the plate.

"Cleanse your palate with some milk," she said, and she went to the propane-powered fridge and pulled out a bottle of fresh milk. She poured him a glass and slid it across the table. He took a sip, rinsing the sweetness out of his mouth.

They started the tasting again, and Zaac realized that he was enjoying having her serious, undivided attention focused on him. There was no flirtation. There was no risk of kissing her—that was for sure and certain—but it was nice just having her ask his opinion, to spend time together.

"Try this one." He held out half a chip that had just butterscotch on it, and she accepted it from his fingers and put it into her mouth, chewing thoughtfully.

"It's good," she said after a moment, "but I think I like the layers of flavor better. What about you?"

"*Yah*, it's very good. I guess Aent Esther Mae is the one to decide, though."

"I hope she likes it."

"Aent Esther Mae isn't the kind of woman to turn down a good idea because it wasn't hers," Zaac said.

"No, she's not," she agreed. "But I'm wondering if this is even a good enough idea."

"I think so." He nodded toward the box of caramel-cashew creams. "Have you shown her those yet?"

She shook her head. "I was still getting up my courage."

"Well, let her taste them. Those are delicious, too. And if there's one thing I've learned from my *aent*, it's that presentation is half the sale. If you can arrange them in an artful way in a pretty box, they'll sell. They're good, Miriam."

"I have to start somewhere, right?" she said. "I don't want to be Esther Mae's competition, but maybe I could prove myself as a candy maker. That would be fun, and I'm just overflowing with ideas."

"Your eyes sparkle when you talk about making candy," he said.

She dropped her gaze, self-conscious, and he wished he hadn't said it. But she did look happier than she'd looked in literally years. That was worth protecting.

"It makes me happy," she said. "There is more than one way to move a life forward, and I think I've found my path."

Yah, there was more than one way to step forward. She was inspiring.

Ivy lifted her head a little bit and dropped it back down

against Zaac's shoulder, and he turned his attention to the baby and patted her diaper. He stood up and started to pace with her as Miriam set about dipping a few more chips.

"Did I hear some taste-testing happening in here?" Elmer asked, coming into the kitchen. Obie wasn't far behind, and the men beamed with pleasure as they each took a dipped chip and popped it into their mouths.

The kitten lay in a box near the stove, and it lifted its little head and mewed. It was ready for more milk, too. Zaac paced over to the window. The rain was coming down in a steady, sideways downpour, and he let his gaze move over the now familiar landmarks—the stable, the buggy shelter, the trees beyond, the fence. There was a dark blur next to the fence pole, and Zaac leaned closer to the glass. Ivy let out a whine of discontent at Zaac's paused movement.

"I can't quite make it out, but—" Zaac started patting Ivy's back again. "I see something by the fence."

"Something?" Miriam came up to the window and stood next to him. She smelled of chocolate and peanut butter. The rain came down in almond-size drops, blurring their view with mist and howling wind. The worn wheel ruts in the drive had filled with water, as had the lower parts of the lawn, and beyond all that was a barbed wire fence separating the yard from a field. The black mound next to the fence post could have been anything from a garbage bag to a clump of dirt, but when the wind whipped against it, Zaac saw the shape of an animal.

"Is that…a dog?" Zaac asked.

Elmer turned away from his taste-testing, and he joined them at the window. The baby started to squirm again, and

Miriam eased the infant out of Zaac's arms. Ivy immediately settled once she felt Miriam's touch again.

"*Yah*, that looks like a dog," Elmer said. "Look, he's trying to move away from the fence—but he looks caught in the barbed wire."

Zaac squinted against the downpour, and her grandfather came up behind them and peered outside, too.

"We can't leave him out there," Obie said.

They had to do something—but Dawdie couldn't be the one who went into the storm after the poor dog, either.

The kitten mewed again, and Miriam looked back toward the hungry little thing.

"Dawdie, would you be willing to feed the kitten?" Miriam asked.

The mewing came more insistently, and her grandfather patted her shoulder and headed over toward the box by the stove. He dipped his hand inside and pulled out the little complaining ball of fluff.

"You are getting louder, little rascal," Obie said to the kitten. "That's a good sign. Let's get your breakfast. Or is this your second breakfast? Your third?"

But Zaac's job here was clear enough. There was a dog out there in the storm that needed help. He exchanged a look with Elmer, and they wordlessly headed for the door, grabbing coats and stomping feet into boots. Zaac looked over his shoulder, and her wide-eyed gaze caught his. Just for a moment, Zaac saw it again—that tender, warm look that had caught him so off guard in the cellar.

"We shouldn't be long," Zaac said.

She nodded. "Be careful out there."

Elmer's gaze flickered between them, and Zaac ducked his head, trying to hide his own embarrassment. Everything always looked worse than it was.

* * *

Zaac hunched his shoulders against the driving rain. Trees thrashed in the gusting wind, and a bucket bounced along the ground, finally lodging against the chicken coop. He glanced back over his shoulder, squinting through the downpour, and in the golden light from the window he saw Miriam standing there with the baby in her arms.

She was watching him. A shiver that had nothing to do with the driving wind went up his arms. He was being silly. She was probably looking past him to the dog. Not everything was about him, after all. In fact, it had never been about him. Back when he'd been hoping she'd see more in him, she'd fallen head over heels for his brother. But Miriam was like that—loyal to a fault. Once she set her eyes on a man, she didn't even notice anyone else.

Zaac had hoped that whatever was budding between Elijah and Miriam would fizzle out over time, but it hadn't. And so Zaac had done the right thing—he'd stepped back and tried to be happy for his brother. In fact, he'd succeeded in being happy for him until he'd noticed his brother still drinking, still sneaking out to gamble and still flirting with Englisher girls when Miriam wasn't around. And that didn't sit comfortably with him. Miriam's loyalty was a treasure.

Lightning flashed in a jagged crack across the storm-darkened clouds, and the boom that followed made his heart skip a beat. The trembling form by the fence jerked away and let out a yelp of pain. It was a medium-size black dog, completely drenched by the storm.

"I'm getting some wire cutters!" Elmer shouted. "You go see if you can calm the dog down, and I'll meet you there."

That was a good idea, and the older man peeled off toward the stable. Zaac slowed his pace as he approached the dog. It bared its teeth at him and growled, low and menacingly.

"Hey… I'm here to help," Zaac said, and he bent down. He could see where the dog's leg was caught, the barbed wire wrapped tightly around and biting into the flesh. Every time the dog pulled back, he let out a squeal of pain.

"Come on, now, *hund*," he said quietly. "I'm a friend." Then he added in prayer, "Gott, calm him down… Let us help him."

He put a hand out cautiously, and the dog didn't growl this time but pulled back and whined, looking up with big pained eyes.

"I'm going to help you," Zaac said quietly. "It'll be all right. You'll see."

He put a hand on the dog's head, and he lowered it submissively.

"*Danke*, Gott…" Because that was truly an answer to prayer. Gott's eye was on more than sparrows—it was on man's best friend, too.

Zaac could feel the animal trembling under his touch. He'd have to hold the dog still, and that might risk a bite. So Zaac pulled off his coat and tossed it over the dog's back. The animal immediately stilled at the warmth, and it was Zaac's turn to shiver in the slicing, frigid gale.

Elmer came jogging up with the wire cutters in hand, and Zaac put the coat tighter around the dog's body and pulled him forward so that the wire was looser around his wounded leg. Elmer pushed the wire cutter against the barbed wire and squeezed hard. With a snap, the wire sprang away, and they uncoiled the rest from around his limb.

The dog trembled in Zaac's arms as he lifted the animal up. He didn't want to let him walk, because he might just run away and end up even more badly hurt in a storm like this one. With the pain relieved, the dog sank his head down against Zaac's neck and whined softly as they headed back toward the house.

Zaac's arm ached from where the glass had sliced into him, too, and he gritted his teeth against the pain and plunged on. Elmer jogged up the steps first and opened the door for him. Zaac had to come up the stairs more carefully, and as they pushed into the warmth of the house, another crack of lightning lit up the sky. Elmer swung the door shut behind him.

Zaac was completely soaked through from the rain, and his skin pebbled with cold. Obie came forward with an old towel, and he looked between Zaac and the dog.

"I don't know who needs this more," Obie said. Then the old man's eyes lowered to his arm. "You're bleeding again."

"Am I?" Zaac couldn't see his arm, so he put the dog down. He spotted a few drops of blood on the floor. Was that from him or the dog?

Elmer squatted next to the dog and pulled off the coat. The dog's leg was bleeding, too. Just then, a thick, warm towel came down over Zaac's shoulders, and he looked up in surprise to see Miriam.

"Come by the fire," she said, and looked down at the dog sympathetically. "Both of you."

"I'll see what I can do for the dog's leg," Elmer said. "You see to Zaac, if you don't mind, Miriam."

Miriam gave a curt nod, and Zaac followed her past the kitchen table, still covered in differently dipped chips, and toward the toasty, hot stove. The baby lay in the basket, sleeping again peacefully, and he meekly held out his arm as Miriam rolled up his sleeve and pulled the last bit of bandage away from the wound.

"This isn't good, Zaac," she said, her voice low. "I'm going to have to put disinfectant on this wound. It looks like it's festering to me."

Zaac looked down at the cut. The edges of his skin were reddened and enflamed.

"How do you feel?" she asked him.

"I don't know," Zaac replied, and to distract from his injury, he added, "It hurts. Chocolate helps."

Miriam smiled faintly. "You can have more."

She put a hand against his forehead, her expression solemn. She moved her hand to his cheek, then the other. It felt a little too nice to be touched by her, and he reached up and caught her wrist to make her stop.

"You don't seem to have a fever," she said, and some color touched her cheeks. "But I need to reclean that wound."

He nodded, and she slipped out of his gentle grasp and pulled a bottle down from a cupboard. She headed to the sink, washed her hands, and then came back with some gauze and the bottle.

Elmer brought the dog closer to the stove, and the older rancher nodded toward the gauze and disinfectant.

"I'm going to need to use that, too," Elmer said.

For a moment, Elmer and Miriam bent over the medical supplies, then parted ways. Elmer leaned over the dog again, and Miriam held out a hand toward Zaac's arm.

"This is going to sting a little," she said.

He laid his arm in her hand, and she put the wet gauze over the cut and pushed down hard. He gasped as the burning pain seemed to sear all the way down to the bone. He repressed the urge to pull back. The gauze turned pink, then red.

"I'm sorry, I'm sorry, I'm sorry," she murmured, but she didn't let up the pressure, either.

The dog gave a little yip, too, as Elmer cleaned his wounds, and Zaac focused on breathing deeply in and out. Then she released the pressure and wiped gently around the wound. He looked down, and the cut still looked rather reddened.

"That's the best I can do for now..." Miriam murmured. "Let's cover the cut again so it can heal."

She got more gauze and another strip of cloth, her fingers moving deftly as she retied the bandage.

"There," she said softly, tucking in the end of the bandage. She reached for the Tupperware container of caramels and put them in front of him.

Zaac popped another caramel into his mouth and then flexed his hand, testing the bandage. Some blood pricked through the white cloth.

"Stop that, Zaac," Miriam said irritably, and he shot her a rueful smile. He might have done it again just to get her reaction, but that was downright foolish.

"Sorry," he said instead, past the caramel tucked in his cheek.

Zaac pulled his towel a little closer around his shoulders, a shiver sliding down his back.

"You're cold," Miriam said.

"A bit," he replied. "I'll warm up."

Miriam headed over to the stove and pushed another stick of wood into the firebox; then she grabbed the kettle and brought it to the sink to fill up. Zaac suppressed another shiver. He was feeling colder than he'd expected to, and he leaned a little closer to the stove.

"Some hot tea will help. I'll put some honey in it," Miriam said, and she cast him a worried look.

"*Danke*. I think tea will be just what I need," he said, and he gave her a reassuring smile. He'd be fine, he was sure. This arm of his would heal up, and he'd probably have a scar, but he'd also have a story to go with it. Besides, if that shard of glass hadn't landed in his arm, it would have landed in Miriam. This was better by far. Still, he didn't want her to worry about him.

Just as she put the kettle on the stove, Ivy started to cry again, and Miriam went over to the basket and lifted the baby out. She looked down at the little one with a sad smile on her face.

"I shouldn't get attached to her, should I?" Her voice was quiet and low, as if her words weren't really intended for him at all.

She pressed a gentle kiss against the baby's head and pulled her close. She closed her eyes, and for a moment, her face looked so utterly peaceful that it brought a lump to Zaac's throat. Then Miriam sighed.

"Zaac, can I get you to sit by the stove and hold the baby? I'll get her bottle," Miriam said.

"I can get the bottle," he said, starting to stand.

"Nonsense." Miriam put the blanket over Zaac to protect the little one from his wet shirt, then laid Ivy on top of the blanket.

She was running away; he could feel it. She wanted to be the one holding the baby, but instead she was asking him to do it…

"Miriam, I think you should be the one who holds her. She wants you, anyway," he said, adjusting the little one in his arms.

"I can't," she said, tears standing in her eyes. She turned back to the cupboard and pulled down the tin of formula. "I'm getting attached."

This wasn't just childcare for her…this went deeper, and she was trying to protect herself from it. A whole lot like he was trying to do with his feelings for her. They were both running from what hurt most.

Ivy started to whimper for her bottle, and he looked down at that scrunched little face.

"It'll be okay…" he murmured.

He wanted to fix all of it—the baby's loss and Miriam's heartbreak. He wanted to go out there and wrestle something. He wanted to lift some great weight, throw some obstacle aside. He wanted to fight some threatening beast.

Gott, show me what I can do!

But the only thing he could do right now was hold a hungry baby.

Chapter Seven

⤬

The rest of the day slipped past. Ankel Elmer went up to bed early, and Dawdie could be heard blowing his nose upstairs. They'd let the dog out to pee, and he'd come back right quick with no desire to run away in that storm, especially after he'd been petted, fed and given a spot by the stove.

The kitten was asleep in her little box, and Miriam was almost certain she had grown again. When Ivy started to cry, Miriam gathered the baby in her arms.

She'd let others hold her a good amount today. That was enough of her own self-restraint, wasn't it?

"Take the rocking chair," Zaac said, standing up.

Miriam sank into the chair in front of the stove, letting the welcome heat warm her legs and arms. Zaac pulled up a kitchen chair next to her, and he leaned his elbows on his knees, his hands folded in front of him.

Ivy nestled into Miriam's neck in that special little way she had, and Miriam snuggled her closer. Ivy wouldn't be here long, but while she was here, she'd feel love.

"Did you decide on which chips you liked best?" Zaac asked.

"*Yah*, the butterscotch and dark chocolate," she replied. "I think I'll call them Lamb's Ears."

She smiled at the thought. They actually reminded her more of a cow's ear, but that didn't sound tasty. There was no real logical reason for it, but Lamb's Ears sounded more poetic.

"What will you do when you leave?" Miriam asked.

"Work a job," he said. "For a while, I'll be learning how to be English, I suppose. But most importantly, I want to join a church that does outreach."

Miriam was silent for a moment, thinking about that. She had never been to another church besides an Amish one. She'd heard about English churches, of course. They had church buildings, and the men and women all sat together in the most scandalous way. Their music was different—downright worldly.

"What kind of outreach do you want to do?" she asked.

"I don't know. Anything they'll let me help with. I've heard that they have an outreach in the city—making meals for homeless people and delivering them. There are small groups that go further—they'll go to a city where there has been a disaster of some sort and pitch in with rebuilding. I could do that. In the summers, they have something called a Vacation Bible School. It's for local *kinner* who might not know anything about Gott, and it's free. They have Bible stories and teach them songs, and basically teach the *kinner* about Gott. It's a huge effort, and it takes countless volunteers to run it."

Zaac explained how the Vacation Bible School worked—how the *kinner*'s parents were likely working or there were busy mothers in need of a rest. The Vacation Bible School was a way to provide some summer activity for the *kinner* and a way to reach the families.

"That sounds really…clever," she admitted.

"They *want* outsiders to join them," Zaac said.

Unlike the Amish. They did their best to keep that line drawn between the Amish community and curious outsiders.

"Aren't they afraid of bad influence?"

"They're more confident of their own good influence." He brightened when he talked about these church outreaches. He'd said her eyes lit up when she talked about making candy, but Zaac came alive when he talked about finding ways to reach Englishers who knew nothing about Gott.

"I heard a pastor talking about the programs their church was providing. They had programs for single mothers, for teenagers, for people struggling with addiction... There were Bible studies, and prayer groups, and groups of men who got together on a weekend and helped older people take care of their yards. He said something I'll never forget. He said we don't have to get on a plane or cross a border to find people who need Gott. They are right here in our backyard. And we Amish—we're closing the gate on them."

"He said that?"

"No, I'm saying that last part," he replied. "But we are closing the gate. We're doing our best to keep them out and keep our own people in. It doesn't feel right to me, Miriam."

Those words gave Miriam an uncomfortable flutter in her stomach. There were parts of the Bible that gave instructions on how to keep a church in order, but he was right that there were other parts that talked about going out to the Gentiles and spreading the good news.

The Amish protected their way of life for a reason. Influence could creep in and change them so that they'd be unrecognizable in a generation. Tradition mattered, but so did protecting their own. Zaac was talking about reaching out—very noble, but what about taking care of the community they had? What about preserving a clean, virtuous, Gott-centered way of life?

Zaac gently touched his bandaged arm, and he suppressed a wince.

"I'm a little less worried about the all the strangers out there," Miriam said, "and I'm more concerned about the people Gott has put right in front of me. Let me see your arm again. I'll get the disinfectant."

Wouldn't it be something if just before Zaac jumped the fence, and just before Miriam embarked on her life of single stability, the two of them forged an honest-to-goodness friendship? Maybe he could be her Englisher friend, and she could be his Amish touchstone. Maybe they could still be something to each other when all this was over.

"Do me a favor?" Miriam said.

Zaac looked over at her mutely.

"Come back and visit," she said. "You'll have all sorts of strangers wanting things from you. But don't forget where you came from."

Zaac smiled faintly. "I couldn't forget you if I tried, Miriam."

His chair creaked, and he leaned over and pressed a kiss against her forehead. The gesture was tender and sweet, and she had to resist the urge to lean into him. His words were gentler and more intimate than she had expected. She realized that she didn't want to say goodbye to him now. Her husband's gruff and stubborn brother had turned into an unexpected confidant and friend.

"I'm going to miss you," Zaac said, and then he pushed himself to his feet. "More than you know."

That night, Zaac lay on the thin camping mattress, his arm aching. He'd said too much. Again. What was with him these last two days? He'd spent years holding all this inside himself, keeping that lid down tight over his emotions. He knew she deserved a man who'd treat her like the treasure she was. And he'd tried his best not to feel more for her than a brotherly admiration.

He had tried so hard…

But Miriam was special, and his heart hadn't listened.

If he'd felt less for Miriam, would Zaac have had more success in reining in his brother? Would Elijah have been more inclined to listen? Because a man might think he was hiding things from his brother, and he might not be hiding things quite as well as he thought. A man could sense things.

Look at Zaac now! Somehow he was saying too much and letting slip too much of what was going on inside him. That wasn't good at all. In the past he could tell himself that if he felt too much for his brother's widow, then at least he'd kept it all under control. But it was starting to spill over now…at the worst-possible time, while he was stuck in her grandfather's home during a storm. He couldn't even leave if he made things awkward!

What is wrong with me, Gott?

He'd kissed her forehead! Another thing he promised he wouldn't even think about doing… But lately, thinking about closing that distance between them had been taking over his thoughts, and then tonight kissing her forehead had just felt so natural. He'd kissed her before he could think better of it. And now he had ample time to lie on this thin mattress and kick himself for it.

He shivered and pulled his blanket up higher. If he was cold, the baby might be, too. He pushed himself up onto his elbow and laid an extra-small baby blanket over one side of the basket. Miriam had swaddled the baby, and he knew enough not to put too much on top of the little thing, so he arranged the blanket more like a tent to hold some warmth in. He had the corner of the blanket over the kitten's box, too. She was curled up in a little ball of fuzz, her tiny side rising and falling.

The woodstove merrily pinged away, and he lay back down. The kitchen was plenty warm. He knew that—this chill felt like illness.

Oh, Gott, please don't let me get Obie's cold, he prayed. There were chores coming in the morning, and there was the baby to be fed…

His arm ached to move it now, and he touched the top of the bandage, putting a little bit of pressure on the wound. The pain increased, and he sucked in a breath. He needed rest. That was all…wasn't it? Just rest.

Overhead, the sound of dog claws scrabbled across the wooden floor. Elmer had taken the dog up with him so that Ivy and the kitten could stay down by the stove, and so far, the animal seemed to be pacing.

"Lie down, *hund*." Elmer's voice was loud enough for Zaac to make out the words. The scrabbling sound stopped.

Zaac closed his eyes and exhaled a slow breath. The baby would wake for her bottle soon enough, and he sent up a prayer for them all as darkness overcame him and he fell asleep to the soft sound of Ivy's breathing and the pinging of the stovepipe.

Zaac awoke when Ivy's cry filtered through his distorted dreams, pulling him groggily into wakefulness. His mouth felt hot and dry, and his arm hurt worse than it had when he'd fallen asleep. He shivered again and pulled the blanket over his shoulders as he sat up and reached for the basket. Ivy squirmed and cried.

He pushed himself to his feet, and a wave of shivers

racked his body. His focus was on Ivy, though. She needed her bottle, and by the look of her diaper, a change, too.

"Gott, give me strength…" he murmured as he forced himself to his feet and headed for the counter. He didn't quite trust himself to pick her up just yet with his arm hurting like it was, and a bottle still to mix.

The stairs creaked behind him, and he looked back to see Miriam come into the kitchen in her white bathrobe. Bare feet padded against the floor, and she bent down and scooped up the crying infant. She shut her eyes and pressed her lips to Ivy's head, and suddenly there was silence.

"Can you light the lamp?" Miriam asked.

Zaac reached for the matches, and they fumbled out of his grip. It was definitely a good choice not to pick Ivy up feeling like this.

"Sorry," Zaac said. "My arm is pretty sore, and I'm—"

He tried to swallow, but his mouth was so dry. The excuse sounded flimsy at best, and he knew that, even past the shivers. Miriam laid Ivy down in her basket, the baby's cries starting up again, and she lit the hanging kerosene lamp, a blaze of light hitting his eyes almost painfully. He turned away from the light and headed toward the kitchen, where the bottle and formula waited.

"Diaper first," Miriam said, her gaze flickering up toward him. "Zaac, you don't look good."

He mixed up a bottle, wrapping his blanket around himself a little more firmly as he brought it back to where Miriam stood.

"Yah," he said meekly.

"Are you sick?" she asked.

"I might be," he conceded. "I think it's just my arm."

Miriam finished with the diaper, went to the kitchen to wash her hands, the baby expertly up on her shoulder, and then came back to retrieve the bottle. But before she took the bottle, she put a cool hand against his head.

"Zaac, you're burning up!"

"I'll be okay," he said.

He'd have to be. There were chores in a couple of hours, and he didn't have the luxury of getting ill right now. If Obie was willing to push past a cold, he could push past whatever this was.

"You said it's your arm?"

Had he said that? He didn't even remember now. He sank into a kitchen chair, and Miriam popped the nipple into the baby's mouth.

"All right, you go back and lie down," Miriam said. "I'm going to finish with the baby, and I'm putting some ginger tea on for you. It helps with inflammation. I'll check your arm. Maybe we need to clean it again…"

She talked on, and Zaac looked over at the thin mattress waiting for him on the floor. He wasn't sure he could get down there very gracefully right now.

"Zaac?" It wasn't Miriam this time, but his brain felt sluggish.

Zaac blinked up to see Elmer in the kitchen now. He was in jeans and a T-shirt again.

"Zaac, you look awful," Elmer said. He marched over and put a hand on Zaac's head as if he were a little boy. "That's a bad fever. Let me see your arm."

Zaac held his arm out, but the shivers made his whole arm shake and he couldn't hold it still. Elmer peeled back the bandage and winced.

"Where is the disinfectant?" Elmer asked brusquely.

There was a flurry of activity then, and Zaac couldn't even keep track of it. Miriam had the baby, but she also rushed around to where everything was. Elmer used more disinfectant on the wound, and Zaac found a steaming mug of ginger tea in front of him.

"Sip it," Miriam said, lifting the mug to his lips. "You need it, Zaac. Take a sip."

Zaac hissed in a breath as Elmer prodded at something in his arm.

"There's a piece of glass in the wound," Elmer said. "Do you have tweezers?"

Zaac felt the dog's head rest on his leg, and he looked down to see the animal's soulful brown eyes gazing up at him. It was his turn to get rescued, it seemed.

Tweezers were found somewhere, and with another bit of painful digging that made Zaac gasp, Elmer said, "Got it," and he heard the sound of something pinging onto the tabletop.

"Now more disinfectant," Elmer said, and with no more warning than that, a cold splash hit his arm and burned like a flame.

"Tylenol," Miriam said, her voice soft and sweet next to his ear, and she pushed two tablets into his mouth, followed by a glass of water. He drank down the pills.

"We can't leave him down here," Miriam said. "He can use my room and I'll—"

"No, no," Elmer said.

"I'm not taking a woman's bed," Zaac said.

"You'll take mine," Elmer said. "Come on. Let's get you up there."

Elmer helped him up. Zaac wove his way to the stairs and allowed the older man to guide him up. The staircase was colder than the kitchen, and the upstairs chillier still, so that by the time Elmer tipped him into the warm bed, Zaac was shaking all over.

"I'll get him another blanket," Miriam said.

She'd followed? He hadn't realized. A moment later, another thick blanket descended over the quilt, and the shivering subsided.

"Another sip, Zaac…" Miriam held the mug, and he sat up a little to take another couple sips of ginger tea.

He sank back into the bed, and his eyes shut on their own accord. He listened to Miriam and Elmer discussing the kitten's need to be fed, too, and as he drifted off, he had the disappointing realization that he was now lined up with the baby, the hurt dog and the kitten, all the ones that needed caring for during this storm.

Ugh. That was not the plan!

Chapter Eight

Miriam sat next to Zaac's bed, Ivy asleep in her arms. She hadn't been able to bring herself to put the little one down. If Miriam was going to be awake tonight, then she might as well hold Ivy, too. Because as much as Miriam needed comfort right now, so did Ivy. Ivy had lost her mother and was in a house with strangers. She was tiny, vulnerable and desperate for love.

Weren't they all?

Tears misted her eyes as she looked down at the sleeping baby in her arms. She was so small. Her little lips pursed in her sleep. Maybe they all just wanted to be loved, and for some of them that goal seemed harder to achieve than others.

Miriam had only ever wanted Elijah to love her, and sometimes he'd expressed his feelings, and other times he'd teased her, or ignored her, or prioritized his Englisher friends and their vices. She'd been foolish enough to think that her love could save the man, but she knew better now. Her love hadn't been enough to hold him back and never would have been.

She'd been hoping that having a baby would bring Elijah home more, and she realized now that had been naive on her part. Nothing would have changed, except that she would have had a child to focus on and fill her heart.

Like Ivy seemed to do…

Maybe this was what she needed—*kinner* to love and care for. And there were plenty of *kinner* who needed a mother to love them well. Maybe she could be the difference in a little one's life—maybe she could start a new path for a child like Ivy. She'd wanted to love and be loved by a husband, but was it possible that Gott was calling her to motherhood on a different path than she'd expected? Could she pursue her own small candy business and be a single *mamm*? Or was she reaching for too much now?

When she'd decided to take care of herself, it had been a relief, and she'd known it meant she wouldn't be a mother, either. But now she couldn't help but wonder if she might be able to have part of her girlhood dreams of a family…a little one of her own and a candy business to support them both.

Zaac's breath came slow and deep as he slept, but the fever raged on. When he awoke, she gave him tea to drink, and she mopped his head with a cool cloth. It was all she could do right now while the storm blew outside.

But Miriam wouldn't leave his side. If he needed something, she wanted to know it right away. If anything changed or got worse, she needed to know…

Zaac pushed back the blanket from his chest and muttered something in his sleep, his words drowned out by the rumble of thunder outside. It sounded like he'd said the word "bishop."

Miriam brushed a hand over his forehead. He was hot still, and a bit sweaty.

"I'm sorry, Bishop," Zaac said, more loudly this time.

"Shhh," Miriam murmured. "It's okay…"

Zaac's eyes opened then, but they still looked glassy with fever, and when he looked at her, it looked like he was looking past her to someone in his dream.

"I wanted to explain."

Silence again.

"No… I have to explain. I have to try…" He muttered something else and rolled his head away from her. "You wouldn't want me to stay if you knew the truth…"

Miriam put a hand on his good arm and patted gently. "Shhh… It's okay, Zaac. Just sleep."

He seemed to be dreaming about a visit with the bishop—defending leaving, maybe? This decision to leave didn't seem to be an easy one.

"I'm not a good Amish man," Zaac suddenly said loudly.

"*Yah*, you are, Zaac," she said with a wry smile. "It's okay. Rest."

He shut his eyes then, and she thought maybe his sleep-talking might be finished, but then he murmured just loud enough for her to make out the words clearly. "I fell in love with my brother's wife…"

Her heart hammered to a stop. She stared down at Zaac's pale face, the stubble dusting over his chin. He didn't have any other sisters-in-law. She was the only one…

"What was that?" she whispered.

He didn't say anything else, his chest rising and falling in a regular rhythm.

"Zaac?" she whispered.

Still nothing. Footsteps creaked outside the door, and she looked over her shoulder. Elmer stood there in his blue jeans and T-shirt. He looked tired.

"Let me take over," Elmer said. "You need to sleep."

Miriam swallowed past a lump in her throat. Would Zaac say more?

Zaac had felt more for her all this time? Or was it just a bad dream—rambling and confusion?

"He was talking in his sleep," she said.

"My son got an infection from a splinter once, and it was like this," Elmer said. "The next time he wakes up, I'll give him more Tylenol, and I'll check his arm. Go on to bed, Miriam. It's your turn to rest."

Miriam laid Ivy in the basket and carried it to her bedroom. She arranged Ivy's basket next to her bed and crawled under the covers again. She let her hand hang down as she listened to the baby's soft breathing.

Miriam's heart still pounded, but now she was worried that Zaac would continue sleep-talking and reveal himself to others. Had Zaac really been in love with her? He'd avoided her! He'd been gruff and distant. Was that to hide his feelings? Was this why he was leaving?

Or maybe none of it was true and it was just a fevered dream.

Then another possibility occurred to her like a boulder settling onto her chest: Would it look like Miriam had been untrue to her husband? Because she hadn't been. She'd been utterly faithful to Elijah. She hadn't even suspected that Zaac felt anything for her at all!

And yet Zaac was now feverish with infection from a gash in his arm, suffered while he'd instinctively protected her.

Gott, heal Zaac, she prayed as she shut her eyes. *And bless him.*

Whatever he felt for her—love, resentment, indifference—he had been her protection when that tree limb came through the window. May Gott be the answer to his prayers.

The next morning, Miriam woke to the sound of Ivy's fussing, and she blinked her eyes open and breathed her morning prayer. She brushed her fingers over Ivy's little cheek, then lifted her up and gave her a kiss. She quickly got dressed, crooning reassurances to Ivy as she pinned her cape dress into place.

"We're going to go get your bottle," Miriam said, putting the last pin into the cloth at her waist. "And change your diaper, too."

She looked toward her closed bedroom door. Was Zaac all right? Elmer had stayed up with him, and if he'd taken a turn for the worse, there would have been some commotion, she was sure.

She shook out her hair and picked up her brush. She brushed her hair—not the slow, long strokes that she usually did—and twisted it up into a bun at the back of her head. She plucked a fresh *kapp* off her shelf and arranged it over her bun, pinning it in place. Then she loosened Ivy's swaddle and lifted her free.

Ivy stopped her fussing cry, and her eyes nearly crossed as she tried to focus on Miriam's face.

"Good morning," Miriam whispered.

In the hallway, she heard the low bass of men's voices… Zaac's voice, too. That was a good sign. She pulled Ivy close against her chest and opened her bedroom door.

Zaac stood in the doorway of Ankel Elmer's bedroom. His hair was mussed and he leaned against the doorframe as if he needed the support, but there was color in his face again. The dog sat on his haunches between Zaac and Elmer, his tail thumping the floor.

"I'm feeling better," Zaac said. "And my arm has stopped aching, too."

"Thank Gott for that." Elmer lifted the bandage and looked underneath it. "*Yah*, looking much better now. The inflammation is fading."

"Thank Gott," Miriam said, and Elmer turned. "I was praying for that."

"Me, too," Elmer said. He patted Zaac on the shoulder. "Now you need some rest. I'll do the chores myself."

"Nonsense," Dawdie said, coming up the stairs, the kitten in his hands. "I'm much better than I was with my cold. We'll do the chores together, *sohn*."

The morning started as it always did, with jobs to do, a fire to stoke up and a hot mug of coffee to drink. Soon enough, Dawdie and Ankel Elmer tramped outside into the steadily falling rain, leaving their empty coffee mugs on the table. The door slammed shut behind them.

Miriam leaned her cheek against Ivy's downy head.

"Can I hold her?" Zaac asked.

Miriam looked at him in surprise, then down at the baby. "*Yah*, of course."

She passed the baby into his arms, and Zaac smiled at Ivy. He was silent for a moment, and she wondered what he felt when he held the little baby.

"*Danke* for taking care of me last night," Zaac said.

"Of course," she said. "How much do you remember?"

"It's a bit hazy," he replied. "I think I tried to feed the baby, didn't I?"

"You put in a good effort," she said with a wry smile. "But you were in no condition. There was a shard of glass in your arm still, and it was festering. Elmer got it out."

"*Yah*, I remember him digging it out rather clearly." But a smile touched his lips. "I don't remember anything after that."

"Elmer got you into the bed in his room, and we took turns sitting with you."

He frowned slightly. "I seem to remember you sitting by the bed. I thought I dreamed it."

"*Nee*. That wasn't a dream. I was there. You talked in

your sleep," she said, trying to sound casual and carefree, and she turned back toward the kitchen again.

"What did I say?"

Miriam looked over her shoulder and found his dark gaze locked on her uneasily. He looked vulnerable, like he was waiting to be chastised, and suddenly saying it out loud felt wrong. Whatever he'd said when he was ill and mumbling should be allowed to stay private. If a man couldn't have privacy when he was sleeping, when could he? Those words hadn't been meant for her... They hadn't been meant for anyone.

"Mostly just muttering," she said, turning back to the cupboard and pulling down a container of oatmeal. "I'm glad you're feeling better, Zaac. I was worried about you. We all were."

"Oh... I had a lot of jumbled dreams last night," he said.

"I think that happens when people are sick," she replied.

"I dreamed about you." He frowned again.

"Oh... Really?" She held her breath.

"We were making chocolates at the Black Bonnet," he said. "We were making sea-salt caramels, and you were doing it wrong."

Miriam laughed. "I was doing it wrong? I can make those with my eyes shut."

"*Yah*. Well, in my dream you wouldn't listen to me. I kept telling you we had to temper the chocolate more, and you kept dipping the caramels into this lumpy chocolate, and..."

"And?" she prompted.

Some color touched his cheeks. "It doesn't matter. It was a frustrating dream is all."

"Sorry about that," she said.

"Not your fault," he said. "In real life, you make phenomenal chocolates. I was obviously just arguing with myself."

"Obviously." She shot him a teasing grin, but then it slipped from her lips. Did he remember his dream about visiting the bishop? Did he remember his confession?

Ivy's fussing pulled Zaac's attention away, and he put her up onto his shoulder. He angled himself toward the stove, and the baby dropped her head down. He rubbed her back gently, and she settled.

"You're good with her, you know," Miriam said.

Zaac's gaze met hers. "Maybe she knows we're the ones who rescued her."

"I wonder if the bishop would let me keep her," Miriam said softly.

Zaac froze, his eyes locked with hers, and she thought of his dream—the one they wouldn't speak of. He'd dreamed of the bishop, too.

"I mean…" She felt heat bloom in her cheeks. This wasn't about his dream, though. "I mean… No, I do mean it. If I'd had my own baby, I'd be raising her. Maybe I could simply…raise Ivy."

"Alone?" he asked.

"*Yah.* I'd be alone if my own baby had lived."

"You could ask," Zaac said. "The bishop is an understanding man."

"*Yah…*" Miriam dropped her gaze. She swallowed, and for a moment she could think of nothing to say, and the silence stretched between them uncomfortably.

"Miriam, did I—" Zaac started, then licked his lips. "Did I say anything strange in my dreams last night?"

"When people talk in their sleep, it's always strange," Miriam said. "My little sister once told me in her sleep that the buckets wouldn't fit on her feet. I mean…dreams are just a tangle of emotions and memories, and fears and hopes. Sometimes they include buckets." She smiled faintly.

"But more importantly, they are private. And whatever you dreamed, it was just that—a tangle of things in your head, all heated up by a fever. You don't owe me any explanations."

Besides, whatever he'd felt for her back then, he'd hidden it rather well. His dreams were his own. He'd also dreamed about making chocolates, hadn't he?

Just a tangle of things, she told herself, but she couldn't help but feel a little bit flustered to have been in his dreams at all.

"I'll get breakfast started," she added.

It was easier than admitting what she'd heard. She didn't want to hear his explanation. And maybe, more acutely, she didn't want to hear him deny it. Not just yet, at least.

Zaac tried to calm his own galloping heartbeat as Miriam headed back to the counter, her back to him. What *had* he said in his sleep? He was grateful Miriam was willing to forget it, but there was one rather poignant dream that had floated to the surface, one that hadn't been a mix of nonsense. In his dream, he'd sat down with the bishop in the quiet office space in his house. He'd had a mug of ginger tea between his hands, and the bishop had shut the door and sat down opposite him.

"What can I do for you, *sohn*?" the older man had asked quietly, and Zaac had opened his heart.

It had been logical, and comforting, and the bishop had given him some advice...

No, it wasn't a nonsense dream at all, and now he feared that he'd been talking in his sleep while he'd been unburdening himself to his spiritual adviser, and that was a frightening thought. He'd admitted to things in that dream he would never admit in real life. He'd told the bishop about his feelings for Miriam.

Ivy's eyes drifted shut, and Zaac eased her down in her basket, close enough to the stove to be cozily warm. Then he pushed himself to his feet.

"I'll set the table," Zaac said.

"Danke." She cast him a smile and turned away again.

What *had* he said in his sleep? How much had he revealed?

The side door opened, and Elmer came in from the mudroom, followed by his father a moment later, both wet from the weather. Zaac was grateful to see them, all the same.

"Did you do the stable chores yet?" Zaac asked.

"Not yet," Elmer replied.

"I can do them, then," Zaac said. "I'm feeling a lot better."

Besides, he wanted to get out and sort through his thoughts.

Obie pulled out a handkerchief and wiped his nose, clearing his throat. Elmer, who had gathered up the kitten, who hung with needle-sharp claws from his shirt, cast Zaac a dubious look.

"I don't think that's a good idea," Elmer said. "As of a few hours ago, you were burning up with a fever. You need to recover."

"Obie was out doing chores, and he's—" Zaac started, but when Obie fixed him with a no-nonsense look, the words evaporated. He was going to say that Obie was an old man, but that suddenly didn't seem wise. "He's recovering, too."

"Which is why he's going to park himself in front of that stove," Elmer said. "I'll do the stable myself after breakfast."

"I don't know what we would have done if you didn't come to visit, Ankel Elmer," Miriam said earnestly.

"Gott works in mysterious ways," Elmer replied. "I'm glad I came when I did."

Gott was providing, indeed, Zaac silently agreed. Elmer had brought more than his help around the farm. He'd also come with the advice that Zaac needed in order to take his next step in going English. There would be no more need to plan, no more need to procrastinate. He'd wanted to get away from this place and start atoning for his guilt, and now Zaac could do just that. He knew that leaving Miriam behind would be difficult, but it would be good for him, too. And better for her. His feelings for her weren't her problem, and he had to make sure it stayed that way.

Miriam set a dish of fried potatoes onto the pot holder in the center of the table and cast Zaac a smile so sweet that his heart tumbled in response.

When Zaac left, he wouldn't see her again for a very long time, and he'd grown accustomed to watching out for her. He didn't even think about it anymore; it had become such an integral part of him. He'd thought that by doing this silently and from a distance that he was keeping those boundaries around his heart firm, but he wasn't so sure about that anymore. His boundaries were crumbling.

Everyone took their places around the table. The baby slept on in her basket and the dog lay down next to her, his nose aimed toward Ivy protectively. He seemed to sense that he had something he could contribute here, too.

"Let's bow our heads," Obie said.

And they all bowed their heads for a silent grace.

Thank you for your provision, Gott, Zaac prayed in his heart. *Now give me the bravery to step out and do what I must... And please, Gott, provide for Miriam where I can't. Provide where I wish I could...*

Because Zaac found himself wishing he had a kitchen of his own, where Miriam could be happily cooking and dipping chocolates and ordering him about. And maybe a cellar of his own where he could finally steal that kiss…

A knock on the door interrupted the dishing up, and the dog let out a low woof. Zaac pushed back his chair. He needed the brief escape anyway.

"I'll get it," he said.

He pulled open the door, and a clean-shaven young Englisher man stood there, his shoulders hunched up and a brown cowboy hat shielding his face from the driving rain. He wore jeans and a brown oilskin coat.

"Good morning," the man said. "I'm sorry to interrupt, but I was hoping—"

The dog let out a puppylike yip and dashed for the door. He obviously recognized this man.

"Come in, come in," Zaac said.

The man came inside, dripping all over the floor, and Zaac shut the door after him. The Englisher squatted down as the dog lunged into his arms. Now inside, Zaac could get a better look at him. He looked to be in his late twenties.

"There you are, Beau," the man said, scratching the dog behind the ears. He stopped at the bandaged leg. "He's hurt?"

"He got tangled in a fence," Zaac said. "We had to cut him free and bandage him up. We didn't know who he belonged to."

"Thank you so much." The man stood back up and shook Zaac's hand so aggressively that it took Zaac by surprise. "I'm James Hiebert. I moved to the area a few months ago, and I'm working at Lapp Brothers Furniture."

"Good to meet you. I'm Isaac Yoder, but I'm just a guest here." Zaac looked over his shoulder at Obie, who'd risen to his feet now. "This is Obadiah Smucker, the man of the house."

"Pleasure to meet you, sir," James said, and he offered Obie one of his enthusiastic handshakes, which just about shook the old man off his feet. "Thank you so much for taking my dog in. I can't thank you enough. Beau has been by my side since he was a tiny pup, and I've been driving all over asking at farms to find out if anyone had seen him. I was praying something fierce that someone had taken him in."

"You might want to take him to a vet," Obie said. "Like Zaac said, he got tangled in a barbed wire fence, and we did our best to clean up his wounds, but he could probably use a look from someone who knows."

"I'll do that," James said, and his eyes scanned the kitchen. He gave Miriam a tip of his hat. "Ma'am."

Miriam blushed and nodded back. *Yah*, these Englisher manners were a little overwhelming, but pleasant all the same.

"Lapp Brothers Furniture, you say?" Elmer said, coming over to shake the man's hand. He held his own a bit better. Maybe he knew how to weather those kinds of handshakes.

The two men spoke for a few minutes. James worked in the shop as a carpenter, making the furniture they sold. He was part of a team of carpenters, but he specialized in wardrobes and shelving. Then James nodded toward the door and the storm outside.

"It's actually really nice to meet you folks," James said. "I used to live in Ohio by an Amish community out there, and I was learning a lot about your way of life and your beliefs. I was really impressed. I mean, we all move at such a quick pace these days, and I think we're losing something really important."

"Are you related to Amish people?" Zaac asked.

"No, nothing like that." James's face colored a little bit.

"I just… Your way of life is a beautiful thing. You slow things down, you stay close to the earth, you prioritize your family, and you don't have the hundred and one distractions the rest of us struggle with. You can focus on God and find your meaning in Him. I've often said that I'd love to live like you do."

Zaac looked at the young man a little more closely. Did he mean it? Because plenty of people said that to be polite— a compliment of sorts. But they didn't actually want to join the faith.

"Do you think you could do it?" Elmer asked, cocking his head to one side. When James looked at his clothes curiously, Elmer added, "I was raised Amish, but I'm living English now. So I've gone the other direction."

"I think I could, honestly," James said, and he looked around a little defensively. "I know what you're thinking. You think that there is no way I could live Amish. It's too hard. And it is hard, but I was raised off the grid. My father keeps a bunker stocked just in case the world comes to an end, so I know how to live simply."

"No offense intended by asking if you could do it," Elmer said quickly.

"Do you ever have people join your community who convert?" James asked.

That was another rather pointed question, and Zaac wondered how serious this Englisher was about an Amish life.

"*Nee*, it hasn't happened," Obie said slowly. "You have to understand, James, that it's more than just learning to live without modern conveniences. It's our faith, our language, our culture. I have heard of a few people who have done it, but none in our community."

"They give up?" James asked.

"From what I heard, *yah*. We've not had anyone try here,

so I haven't seen it firsthand," Obie said. "Joining the faith is a sober and difficult path. The Amish life isn't one that many people are called to."

"It's a beautiful life, though," James said. "I've been simplifying over the last few years, and it's really making a difference in my spiritual walk. I haven't made a cut with electricity yet, though. That's a big step."

"So you're trying to cut the fancy things from your life?" Zaac asked.

"I'm trying."

"Good for you," Zaac said, and he meant it. This man seemed earnest.

"I'd better get going." James bent down and gave his dog another reassuring pat. "It's nice to meet you. Be sure to say hello if you see me around."

And it suddenly occurred to Zaac that he had a way to get home in that pickup truck parked outside, if James would give him a ride. Maybe Gott was providing the space he needed to think, too.

"How are the roads?" Zaac asked. "Is the highway clear?"

"There have been some accidents along the highway," James replied. "But traffic seems to be moving."

"I wonder if you could give me a ride home?" Zaac asked. "I live about fifteen miles from here. And I could answer some questions about Amish living, if you want."

"Yeah, that would be great," James replied. "Thank you."

"We say *danke*."

"Danke." James grinned. *"Danke* very much."

"The stable—" Zaac started.

"I can do the stable," Elmer interjected. "If you've got a reliable ride home, you should take it. You've got your *mamm* and sisters counting on you, too."

Zaac turned toward the family, and Miriam looked uncomfortably at the ground. Maybe she'd miss him just a bit. But there was no way he was going to think straight with her here.

"Obie," Zaac said. "Would you be willing to house my horse until I can come back for him and my buggy when the storm lifts?"

"*Yah*, that's no problem," Obie said.

"I'll repay you any way I can," Zaac added in Pennsylvania Dutch.

"We're neighbors," Obie said. "Why would I need repayment? I'm happy to do it. He'll be safe and warm until you come back."

Just as Zaac was turning, Miriam's warm, brown gaze caught his, and his heart stuttered to a stop.

That was another reason why he needed to go home to his own responsibilities. Time with Miriam at her grandfather's hadn't lessened his feelings for her. He didn't need to muddle with her emotions any further, either. He was leaving Menno Hills, and she was still grieving his brother's death. What he needed right now was space enough to think straight.

"I'll see you later," he said, his voice pitched low for her ears only.

"I hope so, Zaac."

Zaac, James and Beau headed out to the waiting pickup truck. Zaac pulled the door shut firmly behind him. In a storm like this one, Englisher vehicles were a whole lot safer. As he got up into the warm passenger-side seat of James's truck, he looked back at the window and saw Miriam standing there with the baby in her arms.

That was the image in his mind he'd carried around ever since he was a boy...a pretty Amish woman in a *kapp* and apron, a baby in her arms, and her gaze locked on him and only him. She was his Amish hope and dream…if he were staying Amish.

This wasn't a forever goodbye. He would see her again before he left—he'd have to come back for his horse and buggy, after all—but it still stung like something more.

Gott, help me to stop feeling this way about her.

At this point, he'd just be another Yoder brother to break her heart. She deserved a good Amish farmer. This was the same prayer he'd been praying for months, and he had to trust that Gott would answer him.

Chapter Nine

Dawdie and Ankel Elmer finished their breakfast, and Miriam went back to the window, watching the rain pelt down. Zaac was gone—quickly as that. These sudden feelings of sadness didn't make sense. He'd helped them for a couple of days. She'd nursed him through a fever. She'd seen the man in Zaac Yoder...a very dangerous thing, it turned out, because now her emotions were all in a tangle. And it didn't make sense! Zaac was her surly brother-in-law. She used to know how to mentally file him. But now, in a matter of days, he'd become something more to her...a friend, a confidant, someone who understood her plans for the future and hadn't called her misguided or naive.

"I know that young Isaac Yoder is considering leaving the faith," Dawdie said, putting down his fork. "My hearing is better than you seem to think. His *mamm* will be utterly bereft if he leaves the community."

"It wasn't my business to share his decision," Elmer said. "Besides, he isn't baptized yet. He wouldn't be shunned. He can come back to visit," Elmer said quietly. "Like I do."

Dawdie turned away.

"Daet, I visit!" Elmer said. "I come see you. I care. You know that."

"Your mother and I were devastated when you left." The old man turned back. "And I still am. You know Gott gave us this faith and this way to live. Isaac's mother will grieve the same way we did."

Miriam swung her weight back and forth, rocking Ivy.

"My life is not so worldly as you think, Daet," Elmer said quietly. "*Yah*, I use electricity and I drive a truck. That's true, but I am a good Christian. I love my wife and treat her with kindness and respect. I've been married for thirty years, and she has filled my heart that entire time. There are marriages here in Menno Hills that fall very short of the ideal, Daet. You know it as well as I do."

Miriam's breath caught. Marriages like her own… where a husband wasn't completely devoted to his wife, where he didn't live a Christian lifestyle even though he was Amish. In her marriage, she'd had to pray earnestly that Gott would somehow stop her husband from gambling away all his hard-earned money before they could buy what they needed. And when she'd tried to talk to him, it had been a heartbreaking fight. Her marriage had not been an example of any kind of Christian ideal! In fact, her marriage had been painful and disordered, while her Englisher Ankel Elmer's marriage had been loving, united and long-lasting. It wasn't supposed to be that way! Staying Amish was supposed to be a protection from those things.

Why had Gott not protected her? She'd been a good girl growing up. She'd been a sincere Christian, and she'd longed for the day when she'd have her own home and family. She'd behaved herself well. For what? For a marriage that had broken her heart and stolen her joy.

She had done the right things! She had made the right choices. How had this happened to her?

"Miriam, I'm sorry," Elmer said, and she realized he was looking at her now. "I wasn't meaning to insult you or your situation with Elijah. I hope—"

"It's fine," she said quickly.

"What I meant was that marriage troubles are not unique to the Englishers, and marital happiness isn't reserved for Amish couples. My home and my ranch are not worldly. They are the result of my hard work and my faith."

"I know you're a Christian, *sohn*," Dawdie said. "I just wish you could have been an Amish Christian."

Ivy was asleep again, and Miriam found herself looking longingly toward the window. A whole lot of pieces were falling together in her mind now—and her heart was filling with unshed tears. She'd done everything right—she'd followed every sage piece of advice given to her by her elders. And where was she now? Widowed, terrified of another marriage and with a lost pregnancy she was still grieving. And Zaac had left for home, and somehow her emotions had turned into a boiling mess. That made no sense whatsoever. He was Elijah's brother. He was leaving the faith! She should simply bid him farewell and carry on with her life. Why was she feeling this?

What she wanted was some time alone, but that seemed impossible to get, with this storm raging and a house this full.

"Ankel Elmer," Miriam said. "Would you hold Ivy while I go out and do the stable chores?"

"Don't worry about that. I'll do the stable, Miriam," Elmer said, starting to rise. "It's okay."

"No," she said firmly, meeting her uncle's surprised gaze with barely restrained frustration. "I have been cooped up in this house for days now, and I don't care if I get drenched and muddy. I just want to get out for a little while. I don't need to be cared for or mollycoddled. I need to get out and shovel something."

Her uncle looked at her in shock, but he must have seen something in her that he could understand, because then he nodded and held his arms out for the baby.

"Hand her over," he said. "Go on out and shovel."

She eased Ivy into his solid embrace, grateful that he seemed to understand on some level. Miriam went to the mudroom and slammed her feet into her rubber boots. She grabbed a coat from a hook—her grandfather's. It was too big, but it would do the job. She plunged out into the driving rain.

The cold slap of the wind nearly took her breath away, and as she looked up into the gray midmorning clouds, a flash of lightning shot like a jagged crack across the sky. She pulled the door shut solidly behind her, banging it harder than she needed to, but a new fury was coursing through her veins.

She'd been a good wife! She'd been a good Amish woman. Where was the reward for her faithfulness? Gott was supposed to bless them when they followed His will, but she'd gotten nothing but pain in return for her efforts. Her husband was dead, as was her child, and the baby inside the house would be leaving as soon as this storm let up.

"Why?" she prayed aloud, searching the boiling clouds. Thunder rumbled in response, but she would not relent. Gott was the only one who could give her answers now. "Why did You take away everything I ever wanted? What did I do to deserve this?"

There was no answer from above, but the wind roared and whisked her words away. She put her head down and marched toward the stable, her face wet with rain and tears. She would muck out the stalls and have a good cry. What else could she do?

With her hand on the stable door, she looked back at the house and saw two figures standing in the window—her grandfather and her uncle, holding the baby up on his shoulder. They loved her, and they wanted to make sure she was okay.

Privacy was very difficult to come by when a woman had a close and united family. Very hard to come by, indeed.

From their vantage point in the pickup truck, Zaac and James stared at the swirling brown water that covered the highway. The rain continued to come down, gusting and slamming against the windshield. The water swirled with sticks and branches bobbing past in a current that led from one side of the road to the other, flooding a ditch and overflowing into a small lake that used to be a field. It was the only road that connected this end of the district to the other.

"I don't think we're getting you home today," James said, putting the truck into Reverse. "I'm sorry, Zaac."

"I think you're right." Zac leaned forward, taking one more look at that rushing water. "Can you get back to your place?"

"I'm the other direction, and we're on higher ground," James replied. "I'll get back okay."

James did a three-point turn, and they headed back the way they'd come. The windshield wipers whipped back and forth on the highest setting, and it was still hard to see very well. So much for getting home…

"So, back to the same farm?" James asked.

"*Yah*, if you don't mind," Zaac said. "That's where my horse is. I guess I'll be staying there a bit longer."

The Smuckers hadn't seen the back of him after all, it would seem, and as they headed back the way they'd come, he hated how good it felt to be returning. Getting some physical distance from Miriam had been the right thing to do, especially considering how he felt about her. There was something about Miriam that had tugged at him from the start, and he needed to get it under control. But the storm wasn't leaving him any option, and part of him just wanted to throw up his hands and say, "I tried!" But he knew better than that. A good man *kept* trying.

"Do you ever let visitors come to your church services?" James asked.

"Of course," Zaac said. "We don't get a lot of non-Amish visitors, though. The service is in Pennsylvania Dutch, and we use the German Luther Bible. So…if you don't understand the language, it might be hard to follow. I mean, people will try and translate for you, of course."

"Ich spreche ein bisschen Deutsch," James said. *I speak a little German.*

"You do?" Zaac nodded in appreciation. "That would be a big help. You'll understand more."

James shrugged. "I used to attend a Mennonite church, and my mother's family was of German descent, so I did learn a bit of German from my grandparents when I was a kid."

"The language can be a major hurdle for people. Personally, I think it would be nice for us to have bilingual services to make our worship more accessible, but…tradition is strong around here. My single vote doesn't count for a whole lot. So if you're willing to learn Pennsylvania Dutch,

.you'd be able to understand what's going on and chat with people more easily," Zaac said.

"Yeah, I want to come."

"We don't have a church building—that's part of our way. We worship in people's homes. This coming Sunday, it's at the bishop's farm—weather permitting, of course. I can give you the address, but really, drive out this direction and follow the buggies. You'll get there."

That trail of buggies all headed in the same direction— friends, neighbors, family, extended family, all going to worship together and enjoy the hospitality of another family… Zaac would miss that a lot when he was learning a new way of life.

James pulled back into the Smuckers' drive, and he stopped by the house, the engine rumbling comfortably.

"*Danke* for the information," James said. "Maybe I'll see you at the service this Sunday, if I make it."

Zaac wanted to say he'd look for him or that he'd see him there, but he couldn't promise that. Instead, he said, "*Danke* for the ride."

He pushed his hat down a little more firmly and hopped out of the truck into the rain. He started toward the house, but then he saw a light shining in the small window of the stable. Elmer was probably doing the chores out there, and Zaac had promised to do that. He'd go pitch in. If he was going to ask for more hospitality, it was the least he could do.

He looked toward the house once more, and as the truck crept back up the drive, no one appeared in the window. What was he hoping—to see Miriam standing there with the baby in her arms, looking like she was his? Because in his head he was starting to connect her and Ivy in a little fantasy of being a family, and that was foolish of him.

No, mucking out stalls would be good for him. Hard work tended to get a man's feet back on the ground, where they belonged.

He'd feel better about asking for another night of hospitality after he'd done some work.

Zaac pushed open the stable door and stopped short. Miriam stood in the closest stall, a shovel in her hands and tears on her cheeks. What had happened in the short time since he'd left?

Miriam looked up, eyes widened in surprise. She sniffled and wiped at her cheek with the back of one arm.

"Miriam, are you okay?" Zaac strode inside and banged the door shut after him. "You're crying."

"I'm trying to, at least," she shot back, and he stopped short, unsure of how to take that. "Where else am I supposed to get any privacy?"

So she'd come out to the stable for some privacy, and he was ruining that. Still, Miriam wasn't a woman who cried often—she'd had a steel reserve through her marriage and kept up appearances. If she had broken now, it was serious.

"But *why* are you crying?" Zaac reached out and took the shovel out of her hands. He leaned it against the side of the stall. "Are you hurt? Did something happen?"

"A whole lot has happened, Zaac," she said, and she took the shovel back irritably.

"I'll do the stable," Zaac said. It needed to be done, and his horse was lodging here for the time being. It was only right that he do it and that Miriam go back inside, where it was warm and dry.

"I didn't ask you to!" Miriam said curtly.

"You don't have to ask me to!" he shot back. "You never have to ask, Miriam."

"Why are you back?" Miriam bent and pushed the shovel into the soiled hay. "I thought you were going home."

"The highway is flooded," he replied. "If you want privacy here, you can have it. But I can muck out the stalls."

Miriam dumped a shovelful into the wheelbarrow, ignoring him.

"What happened?" Zaac repeated, lowering his voice.

"My husband died," she said, straightening again and dropping the shovel tip down onto the cement floor with a clang. "My baby died, too. And I did everything the way I was supposed to. I loved Gott. I behaved myself when Elijah was courting me, and even after our marriage, I was supportive and loving. I was kind and considerate, and in return he ignored me when I pleaded with him to stop drinking. He told me I was stupid and cowardly when I wanted him to stop gambling, and he withheld his affection when he was displeased about anything at all. You said I looked miserable, and I told you I wasn't. But do you know what I realized standing in that kitchen?"

Zaac shook his head mutely.

"I realized I was truly and deeply unhappy in my marriage. I don't want to risk another one. And that is not what is supposed to happen when an Amish girl does everything right!"

Tears leaked down her cheeks. Miriam came toward him, and he closed the distance between them with one stride. He wrapped his arms around her and crushed her against his chest. She leaned her forehead against his chest and shook with silent sobs.

"Why did I end up with a miserable life?" Her words were muffled against his shirt. "I was a good Amish woman. I prayed. I read my Bible. I loved my husband,

and I did my best. That's supposed to be how a girl gets a happy life, isn't it? That's what we're supposed to do!"

Was she asking why bad things happened to good people? Because he didn't know the answer to that. But he knew why bad husbands happened to good women.

"You married the wrong man," he said.

Miriam pulled back and blinked up at him, her lashes wet with tears. His heart hammered in his throat. He was saying too much again. Were his misplaced feelings supposed to make her feel better?

"What?" she whispered.

"You married the wrong man," he repeated. "You did everything right, but Elijah should have treasured you more."

Miriam stared at him wordlessly, but Zaac knew he was right. While Elijah had been flirting with her, drawing her attention, Zaac had been there in the background. He'd talked with her a few times, too, when he'd been able to get a few minutes with her, but he hadn't been half as funny and daring as Elijah had been, and she'd already had her sights set on Zaac's brother. But he'd been there the whole time.

Miriam sighed. "I married the wrong man."

She turned away again, and he felt himself deflate. Even now she didn't put it together and see who that right guy would have been.

"Do you know, Zaac?" She turned back again. "I am so incredibly tired of having to rely upon someone else to provide for me and take care of me. Do you know how scary that can be? When your entire future is in a man's hands and he's not serious about anything?"

Zaac was silent. He didn't know what that was like, but he could see how she had suffered.

"I lost everything, Zaac. I lost my husband, my child, my life savings that my husband squandered. And I couldn't stop him. We were married. What was mine was his. And what was his, he gambled."

"I'm sorry," Zaac said at last. What could he say? He'd tried to stop Elijah, too, and short of hog-tying him, he couldn't.

"I'm not risking my own future again. Elijah gambled away our money, but I lost something much more precious than dollars and cents. I lost my own sense of purpose, my self-esteem, my peace. I'm not going to lose that again."

Her voice had strengthened, and her tears had dried. This wasn't the old Miriam coming back. This was a whole new Miriam, and he liked her. She was strong and smart, and tired of accepting less than what Gott wanted for her. What Gott planned for her.

"Good," he said with a smile tickling at the corner of his lips.

"'Good'?" She raised her eyebrows as if she didn't believe him.

"*Yah*, good," he repeated, and he stepped closer and caught her hand. "I'm glad you won't let a man drag you down again. And I'm glad you're going to stand up for yourself and do something that makes you happy."

"My *dawdie* isn't going to be quite so supportive," she said.

"You might be surprised," Zaac replied. "I know your marriage was painful to endure, but it was painful to watch, too. Those of us who cared about you had to watch you being disrespected, worn down and taken for granted. Your *dawdie* might be a whole lot more supportive than you think."

"I'm going to see if Esther Mae will help me get a

start," she said. "I'm serious about this. I'm going to build something, and I'm not wasting another week holding back."

"I'll put in a good word for you, for what it's worth. You're a good candy maker, and I have a feeling you'll make a really shrewd businesswoman, too."

"You'd do that for me?" She smiled then, meeting his gaze.

"Of course." He'd do anything for her. She had a power over him that she had no idea about, and maybe that was for the best right now. But he'd put in a good word for her, at the very least. He'd go through fire for this woman.

"I'm going to be okay, Zaac," Miriam said, and she went up on her tiptoes and pressed a kiss against his cheek. He shut his eyes, memorizing the feeling, and when he opened them again, she was just so close. She smelled nice, and that splash of freckles across her nose was even endearing somehow.

Her hand was still in his, and he tugged her a little closer.

"I like you this way," he whispered.

"What way?"

He didn't know how to encapsulate it—she was pretty and sweet, tough and determined. She was a bit of an Amish rebel right now, too, and that was more than just attractive. It was a relief.

Zaac didn't have the words to describe this feeling, so he did the only thing he knew in the moment, and he dipped his head down and his lips touched hers. And when she leaned into his arms, his heart cracked in two.

He had no business kissing her! But she leaned into his embrace, and all his reservations just melted away. He touched her cheek, his heart hammering out of his chest.

This was the kiss he'd been trying not to think about, trying not to long for... This kiss, with the woman he'd been trying to protect all this time. But he hadn't been her answer. She'd found it inside herself.

Chapter Ten

Miriam's heart fluttered as Zaac gathered her up closer against him. He enfolded her in an embrace so tender that everything inside her wanted to simply melt into his arms. She hadn't expected his kiss, but she wasn't willing to end it, either.

He understood her…and he liked her this way. He wasn't staying, but she'd treasure this all the same.

Zaac broke off the kiss with a ragged breath, and she blinked up at him. She had never been kissed like that before, and her heartbeat was pattering like a runaway buggy.

"Oh…" was all she could think to say, and he smiled faintly. His gaze still looked a little bleary, and she took a step out his arms as he released her.

That kiss seemed to have both come out of nowhere and make perfect sense at the same time. Except her brain hadn't quite caught up yet. Had that been locked behind Zaac's stony demeanor all this time?

"I'm sorry," he said. "I shouldn't have kissed you like that. It was my fault."

It wasn't his fault. That was something she'd figured out here in the stable with her shovel and wheelbarrow. But it was also out of bounds. He was leaving. She was staying. This wasn't fair.

"I'm not a dish towel to be picked up and put down," Miriam said.

"No, of course not…" He looked a little confused, but things were suddenly quite clear for Miriam.

"I think I've changed, Zaac."

"Are you going English?"

"No."

"Just checking." He smiled ruefully.

"I make my own choices—for better or worse—and… I kissed you, too." She wasn't sure why that distinction mattered so much to her, but it did. She wasn't a woman to be taken or left at a man's whims ever again.

"What does that mean for us?" Zaac asked.

"Nothing." Miriam swallowed. "I believe in this community, and you're leaving it. So it means exactly nothing."

"Just so you know, Miriam, I don't go around just kissing women," he said.

"I know. You're a good man, Zaac. I think you'll do just fine out there with the Englishers."

Miriam slipped past him out of the stall, hoping that some distance would let her head straighten out.

"Also, we never mention that kiss again," she said, turning back toward him.

There was a beat of silence that was broken by the shuffle of hooves from the stalls. The storm was finally dying down, and rain pattered softly against the roof.

"Okay," Zaac said at last, his conflicted gaze still fixed on her. "Can I do one thing, though?"

"What?" Was he going to kiss her again?

He reached out and pulled a piece of straw from her hair. "Let me finish up the stable. I have to ask your *dawdie* to let me stay another couple of days until the flooding goes down, and I need to earn my keep."

Miriam laughed softly. "Sure. Twist my arm."

Zaac grinned and hoisted the shovel. "I'll see you inside."

Zaac stood there, one hand on the shovel and his gaze following her as she pushed out into the rain and let the door swing shut behind her. The clouds had lightened somewhat, and where there had been a driving, howling wind before, the rain now fell in a soft sprinkle. At least she didn't have to fight the wind now—only her own aching heart.

Miriam *had* been a good woman. And she was still a good woman, but things were going to be different.

Gott, please bless my hard work, she prayed silently. *Bless my efforts to provide for myself, and let me be a blessing to others, too.*

Miriam ducked her head against the cold rain and hurried toward the house. Ivy was waiting there, and her grandfather and uncle... At least in the house, she knew her role and what was expected of her. Out there in the stable, faced with Zaac and his soulful, agonized eyes, she felt as muddled up as a full wringer washer.

The kitchen was warm, and the men both looked up as she came inside. Elmer stood with the baby up on his shoulder, and Dawdie froze, the kitten cupped in his weathered hands.

"Zaac is mucking out the stable," Miriam said.

"He's back?" Dawdie asked.

Miriam moved over to the stove and held her hands out to the heat. "*Yah*, the highway is flooded. He can't get home."

Something between them had changed out there in the stable, and she didn't know what it would look like now.

"He's more than welcome to stay on here until he can get through," Dawdie said.

Elmer brought Ivy over to Miriam and eased the newborn back into her arms. Ivy's eyes opened, and she lifted her head a wobbly inch as she looked up at Miriam.

"Hi, sweetie," Miriam whispered.

She'd missed this little one, too, and she exhaled in a shaky sigh. The rain was letting up now, and it would be only a matter of time before Zaac was able to get past the flooded highway…and only a matter of time before social services, who'd be coming from the direction of town and higher ground, came for Ivy.

"I'll go out and help Zaac finish up," Elmer said, and he headed for the mudroom, and a moment later the door banged shut behind him. She and Dawdie were silent for a moment; then her grandfather heaved a sigh.

"Elmer will not be coming back to the Amish faith," Dawdie said.

Miriam looked up at her grandfather. Tears were standing in his eyes.

"Ever," Dawdie added. "He won't return."

"I know," Miriam said softly. "I've come to realize that. He has his life out there, and we can't offer him anything better."

Dawdie cocked his head to one side, not quite in agreement. "He married an Englisher woman, and he raised his boys to be Englisher, too. He told me he can't abandon his family, and they couldn't live the Amish life. It would be too difficult for them."

"That's understandable, though, isn't it, Dawdie?" she asked quietly.

Dawdie clenched his jaw. "I was raised to believe that he'd not make it to heaven if he left the faith."

"Do you still believe that?" she asked.

Dawdie shook his head. "I'm not the one who makes

those decisions. That is in Gott's hands. But my son is a good man. He's a good husband, a loving *daet*, a devoted Christian. He reads his Bible and he does his best to live by it in his English life."

Much like Zaac, she realized. Zaac was a good man, too, and he felt like he had to go out and tell others about Jesus. How could she judge him for that?

"He lives better than some Amish men I know," Dawdie went on. "But he doesn't live the Amish ways..."

This would always be a knot for her grandfather. Maybe it would be for her, too, when her heart yearned after a man who kept dancing over those lines with the purest of intentions. Zaac was a good man—there was no question. But was he hers?

"What do we do when someone we care about deeply is determined to live English?" she asked.

"The only one you can be responsible for is yourself, Miriam," Dawdie said. "You have to listen to what Gott wants for you. And if I know that Gott wants me to be Amish—and I truly believe that with all of my heart—then I have to trust my son to the Gott who loves him even more than I do."

Miriam looked toward the window. What would she say if Zaac asked her to leave with him? Her heart skipped a beat at that thought, but she knew she couldn't go. She was an Amish woman, and she felt in her bones that Gott wanted her right here in the community He gave her. If Zaac was leaving the faith, then he was simply not the man for her.

Miriam smiled sadly. "You are very wise, Dawdie."

"Is Zaac leaving for sure?" Dawdie asked. "Has he determined to go?"

Miriam nodded. "I believe he has."

Dawdie exhaled a slow breath. "And you care for him."

"It doesn't matter, Dawdie," she said. "He's not staying."

"Are you tempted to follow him?"

Was she? Ankel Elmer had proven that going English didn't have to change a man in a bad direction. He was still kind and decent, and a very good husband. But Miriam was done following men to find her future. She had been serious when she said she was building something of her own.

"Dawdie, the Yoder brothers were both rebels in their own way. I married Elijah, and that was a very difficult life. I'm not leaving the faith. I'm not going English. And I'm not handing my heart to another Yoder brother."

Her grandfather chuckled. "Just checking."

Because what good was their faith and their way of life if they abandoned it when the way got difficult? A promise was given for times just like this. She'd stay the course, and she'd guard her heart.

No more stolen kisses!

Zaac heaved a shovelful of soiled hay into the waiting wheelbarrow. The metal shovel scraped against the cement floor as he worked, trying to drown out his feelings through hard labor. Because when he'd kissed Miriam, he had meant it, and finally pulling her into his arms had cracked open a part of his heart that he wasn't sure he could close up again.

Zaac had been fighting these feelings for Miriam for so long, and he was tired of the struggle. Miriam had done everything right—even if she'd chosen the wrong man. Well, Zaac had been a good man, too. He'd been honest, straightforward, moral and a hard worker. He'd had a heart to offer, as well. Had his mother been right when she told him that talking to his brother about not marrying Miriam had brought down Gott's displeasure on him? Sometimes it wasn't the message a man gave, but the jealousy deep in his spirit that displeased Gott.

Maybe this was all just consequences of the same thing.

Zaac pulled the wheelbarrow down the aisle and headed for the hay bales to add fresh hay to the stall he'd just finished, and the stable door opened. He looked up, half expecting half hoping that he'd see Miriam there, but it was Elmer.

"Miriam said you were back," Elmer said jovially. "The highway is flooded?"

He grabbed an armful of hay and carried it back to the stall.

"*Yah*, it's bad enough that we didn't want to risk it," Zaac said. "You can't see through the water—it's brown muck—and for all we know part of the road is washed out. It's better to wait a bit to be sure."

Zaac looked toward the small window and squinted. The constant drum of rain overhead had abated, and he could hear the rush of the eaves troughs pouring water.

"It's letting up," Elmer said. "Finally."

"Thank Gott…" Zaac murmured. Just not soon enough to save him from crossing lines with Miriam. But he couldn't blame anyone but himself for that.

Elmer crossed his arms and waited while Zaac tossed the last of the straw into the stall, and then Elmer headed over to the next stall, opened it and led the horse to the clean stall. It was Schon, Zaac's horse.

"This is a beautiful animal," Elmer said.

"*Yah*, he's strong and well trained, too. I've had offers to buy him, but I won't sell him for anything."

If he left, he'd have to leave Schon in the care of his

mamm and Johannes. Just one more relationship he'd miss a whole lot.

"A good horse is like a good friend," Elmer said. "It's not just about their work. It's their company, too."

"Yah..." Zaac headed into the dirty stall and started to shovel once more.

"Are you really sure and certain that you're leaving?" Elmer asked.

Zaac paused but didn't look up. Was he sure about this?

"James wants to come to Service Sunday," Zaac said.

Elmer's eyebrows went up at the change of topic. "Oh, *yah*?"

"He wants to fit in with us. He wants to worship with us," Zaac said. "What are his chances of making friends and really settling in?"

Elmer shook his head. "Not great."

Zaac sighed. "That's the thing. He's learned some German—that'll help. But it's more than picking up Pennsylvania Dutch. There's how we look at things. It's the nuances of our rules and our faith. And it's whether or not people will actually accept him."

Elmer was silent, and Zaac felt that familiar rise of irritation.

"You know how Jesus said He came for the sick, not for the well?" Zaac asked.

"*Yah*, I do."

"There are all these people who long for what we have, and we have a fence so high that all they can do is peek over it and watch us. We're like the parable of the man who hid his master's money in a hole in the ground. He didn't grow it. He didn't build it!"

"You really believe in reaching out to others," Elmer said, meeting his gaze.

"I do! I really believe we've got to do more, Elmer. I know there is the struggle to protect what we have, but we have to reach out, too. More than we do."

Zaac sucked in a deep breath and leaned on the handle of the shovel for a moment. "So *yah*, I'm leaving. I can't just stay here and be comfortable. It wouldn't be right. And if I stayed, I'd need to make a decision and get baptized. If I changed my mind then, I wouldn't be able to visit. This is the line—I have to make my choice now."

Elmer eyed him soberly.

"Is this where you try and talk me out of it?" Zaac asked after a beat of silence.

"No," Elmer replied. "This is where I offer you a job."

Zaac blinked at the older man. "Really?"

"Yah." Elmer rubbed a hand over his chin. "I've seen some maturity in you that I haven't seen anywhere else. You've worked hard to keep things rolling on a farm you don't own. You've been kind and considerate to an old man, supportive of my niece, who is going through a really difficult year, and you've taken on challenge after challenge with a dignity that has really impressed me. Even recovering from illness, you're here mucking out stalls. You're right—Amish-raised men are just put together differently. I want a man I can count on to not drink or smoke, to be serious and hardworking and to be honest no matter what. Even when it's hard. Even when it's awkward. I insist upon the truth and the whole truth."

"That's easy enough," Zaac replied. It was how he lived his life.

"I thought so." Elmer cast him a smile. "I'll have to train you, but I think you'll be worth the time it takes to get you where you need to be. A lot of my scheduling is done on computer."

"I can learn," Zaac said.

"Good. How much time do you need to move out to my ranch?" Elmer asked.

This was moving quickly, but it was also a direct answer to Zaac's recent prayers that Gott would provide work for him so he could step out into his new life.

"I'll need about a week," Zaac said. "And…"

"Yah?"

"And I'll need help with a few things. I don't have a cell phone. I have a birth certificate, and I have my driver's license that I got when I started my Rumspringa."

He suddenly realized how unprepared he really felt! He wanted to run an Englisher ranch? He took a deep breath. What did he have in his hand? He had a work ethic honed on the farm, he had faith in a Gott who had provided for him so far and he had a job offer that would pay him enough to cover his bills. He had more than enough.

"I can help you out with those things," Elmer said. "I'm a guy who understands all that, remember? For the first three months I want you working as a regular ranch hand to get a feel for the place. You need to understand the work you're supervising…"

And for the next few minutes, they talked about work details. What would be expected of him, how many hours he'd working a day, where he'd eat his meals and how he'd be paid. They worked together on the stalls, mucking them out, refilling the feed, changing water, and then they brushed down all the horses.

The animals had been through a stressful storm, too, and sometimes they needed the reassurance of human touch that everything was normal and all would be well. Schon nuzzled Zaac for more grain, and Zaac gave him a handful on his palm.

When Zaac and Elmer headed outside again, the rain had fully stopped, and the dense, dark disc of clouds sailed away, bringing their torrent toward the west. Just like that, the storm was over. Trees dripped, and birds had started to twitter in the first hesitant rays of low, warm sunlight.

"We should get some more feed out to the cattle by the trees," Elmer said.

"*Yah*, we should," Zaac agreed, and his gaze moved back toward the house.

In the window, he saw Miriam standing there with the baby up on her shoulder. She swung gently back and forth, and she looked so sweet, but she was vulnerable right now, he realized in a rush, and kissing her had not helped with that.

Gott forgive me...

That was why a man needed self-control. His actions affected more than just himself. Gott had been working during this storm, and he'd provided a job. He should feel more grateful right now than he did.

He *was* grateful, he told himself. He was. He was just realizing that when he headed away from Menno Hills toward Elmer's farm, he'd be leaving behind more than his *mamm* and extended family. He'd be leaving behind Miriam, too, and today that stabbed at that part of his newly cracked-open heart.

When he saw her again, she'd probably have a shop of her own, and loyal customers who loved her Lamb's Ears and Cashew Caramels. She'd have employees and people's respect.

"Zaac?" Elmer said.

Zaac tore his gaze away from the window. "Sorry. What did you say?"

"I said I need to charge my cell phone in the barn for a

little while so I can call my wife and get the mechanic out to take a look at my truck."

"*Yah*, absolutely," Zaac said.

"My cell phone is inside. I'll grab it and meet you at the barn, then," Elmer said.

"Sure thing."

Zaac allowed himself one last look in that window where Miriam stood before he marched out across the marshy lawn toward the gravel road that led to the barn, and the cattle, and the endless work that waited on a farm that had just been hit by a massive storm.

Zaac had work to do. This was how Amish men dealt with their emotions—they buried them in work. Had he completely fallen for her? Did he dare look any closer to find out?

Once he opened his heart, it could blow apart all his best-laid plans. And right now, he needed to just put one boot in front of the other until things made sense again.

Chapter Eleven

"The sun is coming out," Dawdie said, squinting out the window. "Look at that. Every storm passes, you know. My *mamm* used to tell me that every storm runs out of rain and the sun will shine again. That's a life lesson, Miriam."

Miriam turned away from the window. "It is."

And Dawdie told her that very same little glimpse into his boyhood every time a rainstorm passed. Her grandfather went into the mudroom and stomped his feet into his boots.

"I'm going to look things over," he called over his shoulder.

He was antsy to get back outside again, and Miriam didn't blame him. He normally spent most of his day outside with the cattle, but she was glad that he was feeling better, too. The door banged shut as he headed out, leaving her alone.

Miriam went over to the window and a rainbow shone through the passing clouds—almost a full arc—and she paused, drinking it in. Trees dripped, sunlight sparkled, and that rainbow shone vivid and strong through it all. She was reminded of Gott's promise to never flood the earth again. But Gott had also promised to never give them more than they could bear, and the last few months had come very close to her own limit of what she could endure.

"Gott, please provide," she whispered.

An hour passed. Miriam snuggled Ivy, fed the kitten and started tempering some chocolate. She wanted to chocolate-coat some of those caramels with the cashew cream and see how that tasted. Once she'd dipped a handful of caramels and set them on a rack to harden, Ivy started to whimper from her basket, and Miriam took the chocolate off the stove and put it onto a pot holder on the counter, then went to go see to the baby. Ivy's diaper was dirty— very dirty!

"We need to take care of that, don't we, sweetie?" Miriam bent down and kissed her little cheek. "My goodness... We've been feeding you very well. You're growing, too."

Ivy's dark hair stood up in a tuft on top of her head, and she stopped whining at the sound of Miriam's voice, her big blue eyes trying to focus. Miriam leaned closer so that Ivy could see her.

"Hello, sweet girl," she said softly.

The door opened and shut, and she looked up to see Zaac emerge from the mudroom. His hair was mussed, and he tossed his hat onto a peg on the wall.

"Your *dawdie* and *ankel* are going to see the herd again. Elmer and I already checked them, but Obie wants to see them all the same."

"He's particular," Miriam said.

"*Yah*, and that's not a bad thing..." Zaac rubbed his hand against his chin. He paused as if he wanted to say something, then sighed. "I said I'd come help you."

"Ivy has a diaper that needs changing," Miriam said. If they needed a reminder of the reality of things, a dirty diaper could do just that.

"I'm not above changing a diaper."

"You might feel differently about this one," she said with a small smile. "But if you'd grab me a couple of those washcloths and get them warm and wet at the sink, it would be a good help."

Miriam unpinned the diaper, and Ivy wriggled with her new freedom. This diaper was an eventful one, and Miriam carefully folded it over to wipe Ivy's bottom. Zaac came back with two wet cloths, and Miriam set to work cleaning the baby.

"I need one of those receiving blankets," Miriam said, "and if you could grab that diaper—"

Zaac reached for a large uncut diaper. Her daughter's diapers… Her daughter's blankets. These were all meant for a baby who'd never made it to her arms. But Ivy was here.

"No, not that one," she said. "To the left. The one I trimmed."

He grabbed the right one and brought both the receiving blanket and the diaper back. He stood next to her as she worked to change the diaper, and when she pulled the balled-up diaper out from under Ivy, Zaac held it gingerly in front of him.

"You're a natural at this," he said.

Miriam bent down to carefully pin the diaper, keeping her fingers between the baby's soft belly and the diaper pin as she worked. A natural? Maybe. She was a mother who'd never gotten to hold her child.

"I was ready for this…" she replied quietly.

She'd been preparing for this very honor as soon as she'd discovered she was pregnant. She'd been thinking about names, about clothing, about baby supplies and about cuddling her little one. Her heart was ready to wrap around her baby and never ever let go. She was like a mare they'd once had that had lost a foal and had another orphan put in her care. Maternal instinct was strong. Miriam knew Ivy wasn't hers, but somehow it didn't matter. She needed to love Ivy as much as Ivy needed love. Mothers and babies—sometimes they were brought together out of necessity instead of the usual path.

Miriam lifted Ivy out of the basket and settled her against her chest. The baby lifted her head a few times, bobbing her head up as she tried to look around, then dropping her cheek back to Miriam's chest again.

"If you wash your hands, I've dipped some of those caramel-cashew creams to see how they taste with a chocolate coating," she said.

Zaac went to the sink and washed his hands thoroughly. Then he picked up a chocolate and took a careful, chewy, creamy bite.

"Mmm…" He nodded a couple of times. "This is good."

"Better with the chocolate or without?" she asked seriously.

He cast her a grin. "With."

"Okay, *danke*."

"One day I'm going to come buy a box of these at Black Bonnet—or your own shop—and I'm going to call you *ma'am*."

"Just to be obstinately English?" she asked with a low laugh.

"Yup." That was an English way of talking, too, but she shook her head and chuckled.

Zaac picked up a chocolate and held it in front of her lips. "Open."

She complied and he placed the chocolate on her tongue. She chewed slowly, suddenly feeling self-conscious with him watching her expression so closely.

"These are very good," she agreed as she swallowed.

"See?" He nodded. "I'll be buying these by the box."

In his little glimpse into the future, she was an Amish shopkeeper and he was an Englisher rancher coming to buy from her. Worlds apart, and that realization suddenly stung, and she felt tears mist her eyes.

"Are you all right?" he asked.

"Uh-huh." She turned away, blinking back the emotion. "If you call me *ma'am*, I'll charge you double."

"Worth it." There was a smile in his voice.

He was thinking of visiting her, and that was sweet. But somehow she could feel that when they parted ways this time, it was going to be goodbye.

That afternoon, Zaac helped with what chores he could, but Obie and Elmer were happy working together as a father-and-son team, and trailing after them all the time just felt like intruding. So Zaac headed back inside. He needed to be at home working the family land, not sitting around feeling useless.

When he came tramping back in, he found Miriam working with her pots of melted chocolate again. She had a smear of chocolate on one sleeve, and she didn't seem to notice it. Somehow, he found it endearing—this sweet, solitary work of hers.

She was rolling some balls of peanut butter nougat between her hands and dipping them in chocolate. The baby was asleep in her basket, making little sucking motions with her mouth. He stopped to look down at Ivy, and he felt a swell of tenderness toward this little girl. She was so very small, and already her life was so very complicated.

"Do you need a hand?" he asked.

Miriam looked up and a smile touched her lips. "Not really. I'm just playing with an idea."

This really did make her happy, and he was glad to see that. His brother had drained the life out of this woman, and seeing her energy and color coming back made him feel better. She'd had a tough, short marriage, but she was recovering.

She dipped another nougat ball and placed it on a rack. Chocolate dripped onto some parchment paper beneath. Ivy started to whine, and Miriam looked over her shoulder. She made a soft shushing sound.

"It's okay, sweetie pie," Miriam crooned. "I'm here. You sleep."

But Miriam's reassurances only seemed to make Ivy less happy about staying in her basket bed, and she opened her mouth and started to cry. Miriam's fingertips were chocolate coated, and she looked around anxiously.

"Don't worry about it, I've got her," Zaac said. What was he going to do, just sit here and watch Miriam dashing around?

Zaac scooped Ivy up, and the baby looked at him in surprise, eyes wide when he brought her close enough that she could see him.

"You weren't expecting me, huh?" he asked with a low laugh. "Hi there."

He nestled Ivy against his chest and softly patted her rump. She continued her crying—not a real wail, just an expression of her dissatisfaction.

"You don't mind?" Miriam asked. "I think she wanted me."

"Of course not," he said. "She definitely wanted you, but you're busy, Miriam. Your chocolates matter. And I'm an able-bodied man who can be comforting." He looked down at Ivy. "Right?"

Miriam chuckled, and her cheeks pinked a little at that,

and she turned back to her work with the chocolate. Zaac paced up and down the kitchen, murmuring softly to the baby. Then he remembered an old lullaby his *mamm* used to sing when he was little. She sang it now to his nieces and nephews when they came to stay the night. It was a little song with a pretty little tune that he was relatively sure she'd made up herself. But it had comforted him. Maybe it would work for Ivy. He hummed a few bars, trying to remember the words. But as he hummed, Ivy seemed to settle. That meant he couldn't stop, so he started to sing to her quietly.

"Lullaby, go to sleep, you are Gott's little baby. Lullaby, go to sleep, Gott will keep you safe from harm…"

It worked! Zaac felt an elated sense of victory as Ivy settled against his chest and heaved a deep sigh. Her crying stopped, and when he looked down at her, he could see that she wasn't sleeping. She was lying very still, though, her ear against his chest. She was listening to his heartbeat, he realized, and somehow that got under his defenses.

If only the steady beat of his heart could be enough for this little girl… And when he looked up and watched Miriam dipping another chocolate, her eyes on her careful work, he had a sudden image of them as a family in his mind—the three of them enjoying a few hours together. What would it be like to have Miriam at his side and this little baby girl in his arms, both of them reliant on that steady beating heart of his?

It would feel too good, and he pushed the thought back as firmly as he could. Miriam was his brother's widow, and Ivy wasn't their baby. It was just a make-believe scene that wasn't real.

Getting away from Menno Hills would help him untangle his feelings.

But still, he walked back and forth, letting Ivy listen to his heartbeat. He might not be this baby's help for longer than a few days, but while he held her, she could rely on him. One day, he hoped to have a family of his own. But he was leaving, and if he married and had *kinner*, they wouldn't be Amish. And that thought stung.

Chapter Twelve

The day slipped by as Miriam worked on her chocolates. She finished making her latest creations and then washed the dishes and cleaned everything up. They were tasty—not quite as good as her other efforts, though.

Elmer and Dawdie came back for lunch, and Zaac stayed close. A mechanic came by to look at Elmer's truck, and Elmer and the other man leaned over the greasy engine in the driveway, peering inside. Zaac helped with Ivy, fed the kitten and, after lunch had been eaten, stood next to Miriam at the sink, washing dishes.

Having Zaac next to her was a temporary comfort, but a comfort all the same. He was quiet, solid and dependable. And right now, while they waited for the roads to open, it felt like some sort of purgatory, waiting for a goodbye that they both knew was coming.

Miriam accepted a plate from Zaac and dried it. Outside, she heard the rumble of an engine, and they both turned then. Dawdie headed to the window.

"Who is it, Dawdie?" Miriam asked, but she thought she knew.

"I don't know," Dawdie replied. "An Englisher lady in a car. She's just parked. I'd best go see what she needs."

Her grandfather went over to the door and opened it.

It must be a social worker. This was the visit Miriam had been expecting and hoping to put off.

"Hello!" Dawdie called. "Can I help you?"

The screen bounced shut behind him as he headed out onto the steps. Miriam looked over at Zaac, and her heart clenched. When the screen door opened again, Dawdie came back inside with a young Englisher woman in tow. She wore a pair of dress pants and a blouse, and her hair was done up in a twist at the back of her head, pearls in her ears.

"Miriam, Zaac," Dawdie said. "This is Gwen Winters. She's from social services."

She was here for Ivy... Miriam closed her eyes for a moment, sending up a wordless prayer for strength. Then she headed for the basket where Ivy lay, asleep, and she gently lifted the baby back into her arms. Ivy's legs curled up underneath her as she settled against Miriam's chest.

One last cuddle, just for a little while.

"Is this the baby?" Gwen asked with a smile. "It looks like she landed on the right doorstep, I have to tell you. Thank you so much for taking care of her until the storm lifted. How has she been doing?"

"She's a sweetie," Miriam said. "We've been giving her newborn formula, and she's been going through bottles and diapers like babies do."

"Perfect." Gwen held her arms out for the baby. "May I?"

Miriam had to force herself to put the baby into the woman's arms, and Gwen looked the infant over with what looked like a practiced eye. Zaac's warm hand touched her back—a silent comfort.

"She's grown a bit over the last couple of days, too," Zaac said.

"She's small," Gwen said. "She might have been preterm. But she looks strong and healthy, and that's thanks to you." Gwen looked up then and smiled at them. "You made the difference in this baby's survival, I can tell you that. Thank you for your sacrifice these last few days."

"It was no sacrifice," Miriam said.

"I'd better get her back to the office," Gwen said. "We're arranging a pediatrician appointment and a foster care spot for her right now, but she should be in her foster home by this evening."

Miriam nodded, her throat tight. "We forgot the car seat at the shop."

"It's all right. I brought one along. Would you hold her while I just get the car seat adjusted in the back seat?" Gwen asked.

Miriam stepped forward and gathered Ivy back into her arms. The baby nuzzled into her neck, and Miriam went to the door and watched as Gwen worked on something in her back seat. Then she emerged again and came forward with a smile.

"Thank you again," Gwen said cheerily, holding her arms out for Ivy. And this time, Miriam's heartbeat started to patter in her throat. She didn't move. Did she have to do this?

"May I take her now?" Gwen asked, but her expression grew more compassionate, and she paused in front of Miriam. "Are you okay, miss?"

Was Miriam okay? No, she wasn't.

"I lost my baby last year," she whispered.

"Oh…" Gwen's face fell. "I'm so sorry."

"So Ivy was…a wonderful addition," Miriam said, blinking back tears.

"I'm truly sorry," Gwen said quietly. "Do you have support?"

Miriam nodded.

"We have some grief groups women take advantage of when navigating this kind of terrible loss," Gwen said. "Some Amish women take part, too. You wouldn't be alone."

"I have a community," Miriam said. This was what a community was for—for love, understanding and their solid support while she grieved every one of her losses. This was what made an Amish community different. "I'll be okay. I will."

Gwen gave her hand a squeeze. "Maybe you could put her into the car seat for me, and we'll both buckle her up."

Somehow, that felt a little easier, and so she did just that. She laid Ivy in the car seat and let Gwen do the buckles. Then Miriam leaned down and pressed a kiss against the baby's downy head.

"Gott go with you, sweet girl," Miriam said, and then the lump in her throat cut off her words. She eased out of the car, and Gwen handed her a business card.

"If you need anything at all," Gwen said, meeting her gaze. "Or even if you want to check up on Ivy and make sure she's okay. It might help you to feel better. I can give you an update on her."

"Danke," Miriam whispered.

The car headed back up the drive, and Miriam stood there, her arms crossed over her chest as she did her best to hold all her grief inside her. Ivy wasn't hers…she knew that. She also knew that there were laws to protect abandoned children. That was a good thing. Ivy would be safe…

But all the same, it felt like a piece of Miriam's heart had disappeared with the taillights that vanished down the street.

* * *

They stood for a few breaths, staring at the drive where the car had been. Zaac's heart gave a squeeze. He'd miss that baby girl, and he couldn't even explain why he felt like he should go after that car and demand her back. Ridiculous! Who was he?

Obviously, he wouldn't. Ivy belonged to a different world than theirs, and she had simply been placed in their care for a little while. Sometimes Gott worked that way—for a season, or even for just a few days.

Miriam stood frozen, her shoulders hunched up and one hand over her mouth, and his heart dropped. It was like he could see her heart crumbling right in front of him and there was nothing he could do.

"Miriam?" Zaac whispered.

Miriam looked up at him, her eyes flooded with tears, and he wordlessly wrapped his arms around her. He felt it, too, although he knew she felt it so much deeper than he did.

"Is everything okay?" Elmer asked, coming across the gravel. "Is the baby gone already?"

"Yah," Zaac said with a curt nod, not letting Miriam go. "She's just left."

Elmer gave Zaac an uncertain look. He wanted to help, Zaac could tell, but Zaac wasn't about to back down right now. Not even for Miriam's family. What he wanted was some space with her—this felt private. Personal. Ivy hadn't been theirs, but they'd found her together, and there was a bond because of it.

"It's okay." Zaac loosened his hold on Miriam. "Do you want to take a walk?"

Miriam sniffled and nodded. *"Yah*, let's walk."

It was really the only way to get privacy on an Amish

farm. Obie gave Zaac a nod, and he headed soberly up the steps to the house while Elmer, casting a worried look over his shoulder, went back toward his truck and the waiting mechanic.

"Come on," Zaac said, and he caught Miriam's hand in his and led her out past the house and stable, past the fence and onto the gravel road that led toward the barn. She leaned into his arm, and somehow that subtle gesture made him feel three inches taller. He wanted to slide an arm around her, but he wouldn't dare do that.

He just needed to get her out into some wide field with open sky and make sure she was okay. That was it. He needed to know that Miriam was on her feet, that her heart was somewhat mended and her tears dried. Then he could find a way home.

When Zaac squeezed her hand, she squeezed his back. They tramped along together, the wet grass dampening his pants. They headed up the worn road that led toward the red barn, and he angled his steps around the side toward a paddock. Right now, it was empty. He leaned against the rail fence, looking beyond the paddock to the hills of pasture rolling out in front of them. The storm was moving in that direction, a blur of rain coming down from the dark, boiling clouds. But here, the sun shone, and birds were twittering again, flittering from the dripping trees and zipping down to catch bugs emerging after the downpour.

And yet his chest felt like it was in a vise.

"I'm going to miss her, too," Zaac said.

"Will you, really?" she asked.

He nodded. "I wanted to run after the car and get her back. It's silly… I've got no right, but I felt like it was my personal duty to stand between Ivy and just about everything."

"Me, too." Miriam looked up at him, her gaze searching his. "I thought it was only me."

He shook his head.

But those powerful protective instincts weren't just toward the baby—it had been about Miriam, too. They weren't his family, but Ivy had given him an unexpected taste of what a family of his own might feel like.

Miriam leaned against the fence. "That helps, actually."

"Does it?"

"It means I'm not some grieving mother who's going too far."

"This storm made a lot of things feel real," he said.

Whatever this was between them was feeling awfully real, too. But this wasn't new—he'd been smitten with Miriam for a very long time now.

Miriam looked up at him. "I wish you'd stay."

"Your *ankel* offered me a job." It came out more abruptly than he'd intended, and she blinked.

"What? Ankel Elmer did?"

"I wanted to tell you first. He needs a new ranch manager, and he figures I'd make a good one."

She pressed her lips together. The news didn't feel quite so good to him right now, either. It was what he'd been praying for, and now that he had it, there was a lump in his chest.

"This is my chance," he went on. "I've been praying for this kind of opportunity, and everything just came together. If it weren't for the storm, I'd never have met your *ankel*, and he wouldn't have gotten to know me and seen something deeper."

"So you're leaving."

"I think so." He watched her face, looking for some hint of what she was feeling. "What if you came with me?"

"What?" She eyed him uncertainly.

"Hear me out, Miriam. You've changed. You know you have! You're tired of doing things the 'right way' and ending up in unhappiness. You're not willing to just hand your life over to a husband now. You've got plans of your own. Do you know what that sounds like to me? That sounds English."

"I'm not English!" Fire sparked in her eyes. "I am very much an Amish woman. I've already been married. I'm done with that. But that doesn't make me less Amish!"

And somehow, Zaac knew that, but he'd been hoping she would come with him.

"I can visit you," he said hopefully.

She was silent, and he didn't need her to go over all the reasons why a man who jumped the fence couldn't just come and pal around with a single Amish woman. He knew the rules. He knew exactly what people would think, and if she wanted a good Amish life, she couldn't let him just come by like that.

"If you don't want me coming to the shop, maybe I understand," he went on when she hadn't answered. "I mean, you'd have your Amish reputation to consider, and I wouldn't want to ruin anything for you. But you could come to your *ankel*'s ranch and see me, right?"

"For what purpose?" Miriam shook her head and took a step closer. "Why, Zaac? You'll be English, and I'll be Amish. What would my visit do besides confuse matters?"

"It would make me feel better!" That lump in his chest rose to his throat. "Because I'll miss you! That's why. It would be a comfort, Miriam."

She dropped her gaze.

"Oh, for crying out loud, Miriam! I love you!" The words came out in an exasperated rush, and she froze.

He hadn't meant to say it. And yet, he'd been fighting not to love her for so long that admitting to it was a strange relief.

"I'm sorry if it's hard to hear, but it's true." He searched her face. "I've been in love with you since you started dating my brother. And I know that's terrible. Trust me, I've done nothing but pray for Gott to take it away. I've been racked with guilt. But it's the truth—I'm in love with you. And never seeing you again feels like the worst punishment I could face. I've got practice in holding myself back. The only thing I don't have practice in is not seeing you at all, and I don't think I can handle that."

Her eyes lifted slowly then, and her lips parted, her sparkling gaze searching his as if she was looking for some sign of deceit. She wouldn't find it. He'd never lied to her, and he wouldn't start now.

"You love me?" she whispered.

And the only way he could answer with utter honestly was to lower his lips over hers and pull her into his arms. This was where she belonged—pulled solidly against his heartbeat. She sank against him, and he gathered her up, the toes of her rubber boots pressed against the toes of his. He loved her, and he was so tired of holding it all back. She was his weakness, and he doubted that would ever change.

When he pulled back, her eyes fluttered open, her cheeks pink.

"Please come with me," he whispered. Her uncle might understand, but her grandfather wouldn't. If she went with him, a lot of people would blame him for luring her away, and they wouldn't be wrong.

Miriam mutely shook her head.

"I know, I know…" He released all of her except for her

hand. He couldn't quite bring himself to let go of her all the way. "I'm asking too much."

"I'm not marrying again, Zaac," she said. "It doesn't matter if I love you. My heart has steered me wrong before."

But his heart clamped down on what she'd just said.

"You love me?" he whispered.

"The point is, it doesn't matter!"

"No, the point is, you love me, too…" he said in disbelief.

"I do," she said, tears welling in her eyes. "And I shouldn't have let myself. You shouldn't have been so sweet! Maybe you could have continued acting all angry and stony, and it might have helped matters."

"But you do love me." A smile tickled his lips. This felt like a bittersweet victory.

"*Yah*, I do."

"What if I stayed for you?" he asked.

"For what, to maintain a friendship with me?" she asked. "I'm not marrying again, Zaac! You'd be frustrated. And if you stayed for me, how long would it last? Has your conscience changed on the matter? No, for a little while you might stay, and we'd be friends, but I wouldn't be able to court you properly, because I wouldn't be willing to hand my life over to you like I did with your brother. So you'd be unhappy, and I'd be unhappy."

She was right, of course, and he reached up and tenderly touched the tip of her chin. Why did this have to be so difficult?

"Zaac, you believe in helping people, and that's not going to go away. If there is one lesson I've learned, it's that I can't change a man. No matter how much I might want to."

Miriam wiped a tear off her cheek and took a step back.

"What do we do?" he asked helplessly.

She was silent for a beat, and then she met his gaze. "We

knew where we stood, Zaac. Our feelings don't change any of that. So I think you should take the job my *ankel* offered you. It's a good opportunity for you."

"Can I visit you?" he asked.

Miriam shook her head. "It'll only make it harder."

She understood, at least. It might be the only solace he'd get.

"May Gott protect you out there, Zaac—" Her lips wobbled, and she turned then and walked briskly back toward the house. He wanted to call to her, but what solution could he offer? He'd already given every option he could think of. After a few steps, she pulled up her skirt and broke into a jog.

Zaac stood there, his heart in his throat, and cast his eyes up at the sky and the glittering sunlight. What was he supposed to do with that? She loved him. He loved her—oh, how he loved her! And there still wasn't an answer.

He walked slowly back toward the house as Miriam disappeared inside. Elmer dropped the hood on his truck shut, and the engine rumbled to life.

The mechanic hopped out of the truck and wiped his hands.

"It's running!" Elmer called to Zaac. "Do you need that ride home?"

Maybe the water covering the highway would be lower now. But all Zaac knew was that he couldn't stay here any longer.

"*Danke*, I'll take that ride," Zaac said, but his voice sounded tight in his own ears. Elmer gave him a concerned look, but the older man nodded all the same.

"Did you want to go say goodbye to Miriam?" The way Elmer said the words made them sound rather loaded, but a goodbye would only make things worse.

"No, I've said all I can," he said. "I'd better get home."

It was the safest choice by far, but his heart still felt like it was beating through tatters. He'd loved her without hope for so long now that he wasn't sure his heart could learn to do anything else.

Chapter Thirteen

Tears blurred Miriam's eyes as she let the screen door bounce shut behind her. Her grandfather stood in the middle of the kitchen, watching her with a look of surprise, with the kitten formula in one hand and the kitten in the other.

"Miriam?" he called.

But she didn't stop, or trust herself to answer. She stumbled up the stairs and shut her bedroom door behind her. She leaned against the cool wood, covering her face with her hands.

Whatever had just happened during this storm, she had fallen in love again. And it was ridiculous, because she had no intention of handing her life over to another man. It was too big a risk. She would not leave her ability to eat and plan for her future in anyone else's hands again! If she'd learned anything in her short marriage, it was just how vulnerable a woman could be. She loved Zaac. She wanted him to be happy, and she wished she could be part of making him happy, but marrying him? No. Never again.

And yet, mixed in with her grief about Zaac were all the other emotional wounds of the last year. Her marriage, her husband's death, the loss of her child… And less than an hour ago, she'd handed over a warm, wriggling newborn she'd fallen desperately in love with to a government official. Ivy wasn't the baby girl she'd prepared for, but she'd loved her all the same. Miriam wasn't ready to go through this grief all over again.

She sank onto the edge of her bed and pulled up the edge of the quilt to dab at her eyes.

"Gott, I love him…"

She didn't love the man she believed he could become. This time, she loved the man just as he was. She didn't love his potential, she loved his character. But that didn't mean she could trust him with her future, or that she could leave her Amish life for him.

A prism hung from the clasp on her bedroom window, and it reflected little rainbow-colored patterns along her wall. Rainbows…the promise that Gott would not destroy the earth again. What she wouldn't give for a promise from Gott Himself that she could love again without hesitation.

But Gott didn't give those kinds of promises. Love could hurt, and there was no guarantee that it wouldn't.

There was a tap on her door.

"Dawdie, I just need some time alone," she said through her tears.

"What happened?" Dawdie's voice was muffled.

"Nothing. I'm okay, Dawdie."

There was silence, and then she heard her grandfather's footsteps heading back towards the stairs.

Dawdie loved her, but Miriam was too broken and battered and tangled up to even hear his advice right now. Right now, she needed wisdom from another source.

Gott, I love them. I love Zaac, and I love Ivy. And I see how impossible that is. I know we can't be a family, the three of us. I know it's ridiculous. But I love them… Can't

You just wipe my heart clean, take away these misplaced feelings and let me finally stop hurting?

It was the only thing she could think to pray.

She put her hand into her skirt pocket and pulled out the social worker's business card. When Ivy cried, she dearly hoped that loving arms were waiting.

The flooding had already receded by the time Elmer and Zaac got to the stretch of highway that had been so problematic earlier. There was still some water on the road, but it was passable in a truck. The drive from the Smucker farm to the Yoder ranch took less than half an hour, and as the scenery whipped past him, Zaac tried to calm his mind. Gott had provided. That was what he kept trying to remind himself. He'd prayed for a job that would tick all the boxes, and he'd gotten one. He'd prayed for a clear path to let him follow his conscience, and what he believed was Gott's leading, and he'd gotten it.

So why did it come with heartbreak, too? Was it some sort of penance? Was it a lesson for him? A punishment, maybe, for having harbored these feelings for so long? But if that were the case, it was hardly fair for Miriam to be punished, too. His wayward feelings for her weren't her fault!

When they got to the ranch, Elmer pulled to a stop next to the two-story farmhouse. Zaac's mother was out in the garden, bent over the leafy zucchini plants with a plastic five-gallon bucket next to her, harvesting the zucchinis that were ripe. She straightened when she saw them drive in and shaded her eyes.

"*Danke* for the ride, Elmer," Zaac said. "And for the employment. You are an answer to prayer, and I'll work hard for you."

"Of course," Elmer said, and he pulled a card out of the breast pocket of his shirt. "This is my contact information. Take ten days, and you can start on Monday the fourteenth."

He climbed out of the truck, and his mother stepped over the rows and came across the grass toward him.

"I got your message from the neighbor," Mamm called. "I'm glad you're back." She shaded her eyes, looking toward the truck. "Is that you, Elmer Smucker?"

"*Yah!* How are you?" Elmer called from the truck. "I'm sorry to rush, but I need to get a few things from town. Can I get you anything while I'm there?"

"No, no, I'm okay," Mamm replied. "But *danke* for the offer, and for bringing my son home."

"My pleasure," Elmer replied. "I'll see you at Service Sunday."

Zaac headed toward the garden as Elmer pulled back out again.

"How did you hold up during the storm?" Zaac asked.

"I did all right. Johannes came by and helped me out. He and Emma just left, actually. They wanted to check over their own property to make sure nothing flooded." She reached out and touched his arm. "Are you all right, *sohn*?"

That was a loaded question, because so much had happened since that storm had locked him in the Smucker home. His mother seemed to read the hesitation on his face, because she nodded knowingly.

"Come on. Let's get some meadow tea and talk," she said, leading the way back up toward the house.

The day was muggy and warm now that the sun had come out, and Zaac swatted at a mosquito that whined around his head. He followed his mother up the steps and into the house. It had that familiar scent of baking and dish soap that had always been comforting. Today, though, it wasn't settling his nerves.

"Mamm, I have something to tell you," Zaac said.

His mother put a tall glass of sweet meadow tea in front of him and sat down opposite him with an encouraging smile. "Go on, then."

She looked so happy, so contented…and a wriggle of guilt nearly stopped him.

"I'm leaving Menno Hills, Mamm. I've got a job lined up at Elmer Smucker's ranch. I'll be—" He swallowed. "I'll be living English."

He expected surprise from her, but she didn't look shocked. She dropped her gaze and frowned for a moment, looking at her hands on the tabletop, but then she looked up again, and she didn't look angry or betrayed. Just sad. Maybe it wouldn't be so shocking to those who knew him best.

So Zaac started to explain. He told her about the missions other churches were so devoted to. He told her about James Hiebert who wanted to come be part of their church but had very little hope of lasting there. He told her how they needed to be doing more. But then other things started to tumble out, too. Like about little Ivy, who had landed on their doorstep, and the kitten Elmer had found in a puddle, and the dog tangled in a fence.

"What happened with the baby?" she asked. "Poor thing."

"We had to take care of her until a social worker could come collect her after the storm," he said. "And we all got attached, I think. Especially Miriam. And me…"

He told the story, but he left out the part where he was in love with Miriam, but he didn't seem to hide it very well, because his mother asked him, "Did you and Miriam come to any…understandings?"

"No. Well…we understand that it won't work."

His mother sighed. "I'm sorry to hear it."

"Mamm, she's my brother's widow," he said.

"Many couples have begun with exactly that start," she replied. "Your brother is gone, *sohn*. He is beyond jealousy. He's beyond pain."

"I know."

"And Miriam needs love and care, too—"

"Elijah might not have died if I'd worked harder to help him." Zaac's voice choked and he stopped, swallowing hard. Because this was a big part of his guilt. He'd let his brother down. He'd gotten tired and frustrated, and he hadn't gone to stop him. The one time he should have.

"Do you blame yourself?" she asked softly.

"A little bit."

"Do you blame me?" she asked, and her warm gaze locked onto his.

Zaac blinked at her. "What? No."

"Because I was his *mamm*. I knew about his struggles, too. Do you think I could have done more?" She met his gaze hesitantly, as if she thought he might actually say yes.

"*Nee*, Mamm, of course not!"

Tears welled in her eyes. "Isaac, your brother wouldn't listen. We all tried. *Yah*, there were times we were able to derail his plans, but we could not live his life for him. We couldn't stop consequences from finding him. All I can pray now is that in death, he found Gott's mercy. But you are not responsible for his actions. You are not the reason why your brother died."

"I might have been able to stop him, though," he said.

"Elijah needed Gott in his life. The only thing that would have fixed his problems was Elijah handing his life over to his Creator. That was all! You couldn't fix him, *sohn*. I couldn't fix him. So stop blaming yourself for not being Gott."

"I was in love with his wife…"

"Oh, Zaac…"

"It's true." He swallowed hard.

"I knew you loved her," she said softly, and he looked up then, startled. So much for hiding it. "Oh, don't look so surprised. I raised you boys. I know you better than anyone. But you never breathed a word about your feelings. *Sohn*, feelings are natural. It's what we do with them that is good or bad. You are a human being. You have emotions! You cared deeply for Miriam, and she never knew. Is that not credit to you?"

"But what if my brother hadn't died?" Zaac asked. "What would I have done then? Gone on loving her and watching my brother be a terrible husband to her?"

His mother shook her head. "No, you wouldn't have. You would have left, *sohn*." Her voice shook. "You would have gone English, most likely. Or you would have found another community. You would have put time and distance between you and Miriam, and you would have asked Gott to give you another woman to love. And Gott would have provided for you. Is that why you're leaving now?"

"Not entirely." He was tired of explaining. He was tired of trying to show the people he loved why he needed to leave. This was why people who jumped the fence normally ran away in the middle of the night. It was easier than facing the heartbreak.

"I have some thoughts," Mamm said quietly. "Would you like to hear them?"

Zaac exhaled a tired sigh. "Okay."

"Besides your feelings for Miriam, you want to leave because you want to help others," she said.

"Yah." So she did understand...

"You want to tell them about Jesus. You want to share what we've got."

"Yah."

"That's noble, *sohn*."

"You don't disagree with me?" he asked, frowning.

She sucked in a slow breath. "Let's set aside if I agree or not."

"Can we do that?" he asked with a sad smile. His mother was normally quite liberal with her opinions about what her *kinner* should be doing.

"Listen to me." She leaned her elbows on the table and fixed him with an earnest look. "From what you've told me about these last few days, Gott brought an abandoned Englisher newborn to the door of your work. He brought you to the Smucker home, where you were able to help old Obie when he needed it. He brought a nearly drowned kitten and an injured dog into your care, too. And then He brought an Englisher who is longing for some Amish connection to the very door of where you were staying."

"Yah..."

"And all the while, He had Miriam in your care, too. Miriam, who is still grieving the loss of her baby and the loss of Elijah... The poor, poor young woman who just needed a strong shoulder to lean on."

"Miriam and I were caring for everyone else together," he said.

"I dare say, you held her together, too," Mamm replied.

"I know her. And I know you. You've been a silent but solid support for her all this time. I've seen it."

"I tried." But helping Miriam in any way he could wasn't a burden, or a task. It was an honor. He'd be her rock from a distance, if he had to. But he would always be there for Miriam, even if he had to temper his feelings down to something more brotherly.

"*Sohn*, is it possible that Gott has plans for you right here?"

Zaac met his mother's thoughtful gaze. Gott's hand was in everything, and his mother had a point. Every vulnerable animal and person had been brought right to him these last few days. It had been so coincidental that there could be no random explanation. Gott had brought them all together, and they knew from scripture that Gott was a *gott* of purpose and reason and order...

"I don't know," he admitted. "I thought maybe my feelings for Miriam, and this completely impossible situation, were a way of purifying me."

"You mean punishing."

"Maybe."

"Pray on it, then," she said. "Because I don't pretend to know what Gott is doing, but I sense His fingerprints on this. And you are a grown man, now. Gott won't tell me what you need to do. He'll tell you. But I can be absolutely certain of one thing, Isaac."

"What's that?"

"When you ask Gott to forgive you for a mistake, for a sin, for not being enough, for letting someone down... When you ask for forgiveness, he forgives freely and generously. If you hold on to your mistake, that's not Gott working. That's you clinging to something that Gott has already forgiven. It's prideful, Isaac. For sure and for certain."

Zaac dropped his gaze. Gott forgave…and Zaac believed that, but sometimes it was harder to forgive himself.

His mother stood up. "Are you hungry? I've got some leftover blackberry cobbler."

"*Yah*, that would be nice. *Danke*, Mamm."

Zaac was grateful for more than the cobbler. He was grateful for her faith and her stability, and her insight and wisdom in the face of his own guilt.

Maybe she was right and it was time to forgive himself. But that didn't mean he was supposed to stay here.

Miriam slept poorly that night, waking up several times to lie awake and cry into her pillow. By the third time she woke up, her tears were spent and she simply lay there, wondering what was wrong with her that she kept falling in love with Yoder men.

She'd prayed and prayed, but Gott didn't seem to be answering her prayer that she'd stop loving Zaac. And he did not take away that longing in her heart to bring Ivy home, either. Bringing Ivy back didn't make sense, of course. She wasn't married. She didn't have a husband to provide for her. She didn't have a home of her own, either, or even more than a part-time income from the chocolate shop, and that job would have to be relinquished if she was to raise a baby. How could she possibly raise Ivy on her own? Loving that baby girl wasn't enough. All she could do was pray that Gott would protect little Ivy, provide for her, and give her a mother would love her as much as Miriam did.

The next morning was bright as Miriam arrived at Black Bonnet Amish Chocolates, but her heart was heavy. She and Zaac would be working together again today, and she wasn't sure what it would be like after their goodbye.

Would he be hurt? Would they be able to be in the same room together? Miriam wished she knew, but all the same, she was looking forward to seeing him. He'd be leaving for Ankel Elmer's ranch soon, and whatever time they had left was both precious and painful.

The bell above the door tinkled as she went inside. The sign was still flipped to Closed in the front window, and Miriam made sure the door was shut firmly behind her.

Esther Mae poked her head out of the kitchen and shot Miriam a sunshiney smile.

"Good morning!" Esther Mae called.

Esther Mae was in her early forties, but she looked at least five years younger.

"You're back?" Miriam said, trying to smile. "I thought I was working with Zaac again today."

"*Nee*, I dropped by his place last night to let him know I was back so he could help his *mamm* get their farm sorted out after that storm. He told me about the baby on the doorstep."

Esther Mae wiped her hands on a towel and came into the front of the store. "I can only imagine how conflicting that would have been for you. Is the little one okay now?"

With Esther Mae's gentle gaze on her, Miriam's eyes welled with tears. She wasn't sure how many times she'd tell this story, but she stuck to the facts—and to Ivy. She didn't want to tell her boss about her emotional complications with Esther Mae's nephew.

"But Ivy is safe, and I can call and check on her if I want to," Miriam said.

"And my nephew?" Esther Mae asked. "How did he do managing the store while I was away?"

"He's a good manager," Miriam said truthfully, but Esther Mae seemed to see something in her gaze, and Miriam quickly shook her head. "I don't want to talk about him, though. I wanted to talk about some candy ideas I have."

"Oh? Now you have my interest, for sure and for certain. What kinds of ideas?"

Miriam and Esther Mae went into the kitchen, and Miriam pulled out some pieces of paper where she'd written down the most successful versions of her Caramel-Cashew Creams and her Lamb's Ears. Esther Mae nodded slowly.

"I'd like to taste these," she said. "Can you whip some up today?"

"*Yah*, I could do that."

"Good. I'd like to see what they taste like, but I have a feeling these are going to be very good. You say you already had some people's reactions to them?"

"Zaac's—and he promises he was being very honest," Miriam replied. "And my *dawdie* and *ankel*. Everyone loved them."

"That's a very good start." Esther Mae smiled. "If you like, I could give you a small section of the display case for Miriam's Creations, and we can see how they sell, too."

"You'd do that?" Miriam asked hopefully.

"Of course."

The happiness of the moment was suddenly clouded as tears filled her eyes. She wiped at her face and turned away. "I'm sorry, I don't know what's wrong with me."

"Oh, Miriam…what happened?" Esther Mae put a gentle

hand on Miriam's shoulder. "Something with Zaac—I can see it all over your face."

The whole story flooded out of her, ending with the heartbreaking news: "...and now Zaac is leaving the community."

"He's really leaving?" Esther Mae breathed. "So...it was a success, giving him the extra experience. A miserable, heartbreaking success."

Esther Mae was silent for a few moments, her lips pressed together in a tight line. Then she circled around the front counter and caught Miriam's hand.

"Oh, Miriam... I wanted you two to work together because I suspected that Zaac felt more for you. I was hoping to make a match between the two of you."

"I'm sorry."

"No, I'm the one to be sorry. I shouldn't meddle. It was wrong of me. I really am sorry to have caused you any extra pain. I just wanted you find happiness—you deserve it."

"It won't work. It's okay, though. I'll get over it." Because it wasn't just Zaac leaving that stood between them. She was afraid to marry again. There was no one to blame, least of all Esther Mae.

Esther Mae seemed to read more in her expression because she nodded as if she understood the heart of the matter and patted her hand sympathetically. Who knew? Maybe Zaac had told his *mamm*, and his *mamm* had told his *aent*... Word could travel.

There was a tap on the door, and Esther Mae headed over, flipped the sign to Open, and swung the door open. An Englisher woman came into the shop—a woman with a short, ash gray bob and an easy smile.

"Miriam?"

"Aent Trish!"

Trish, Elmer's wife of thirty years, wore a pair of blue jeans, cowboy boots and an embroidered teal-colored blouse that drew Miriam's gaze. She hadn't seen her *aent* since Elijah's funeral, and this version of her—colorful, smiling, rosy—was such a difference from the black-clad *aent* of a year ago. Trish came forward and gave Miriam a squeeze.

"It's so good to see you, sweetie!" Trish said. "How are you doing?"

Esther Mae quietly set about filling the display case with chocolates.

"Why don't you two take a little walk for a few minutes?" Esther Mae said. "I don't mind a bit. I can take care of things until you're back."

"*Danke*, Esther Mae," Miriam said, and she cast her boss a grateful look.

Miriam and Trish went out the front door and headed down the sidewalk in the early morning sunlight. The air was cool and still smelled wet and fresh from the storm. The owner of the card shop across the street was sweeping up a tipped-over flower planter, the swishing sound of her broom traveling on the breeze toward them.

"Elmer said it was a tough few days for you," Trish said. "He thought maybe you could use some girl talk."

"Ankel Elmer said that?" she asked.

"He did. Is that okay?"

Miriam nodded. "I don't have my *mamm* to talk things over with anymore. That was kind of him."

"So what's going on?" Trish's pace slowed and she wound her arm through Miriam's.

"I fell in love with a man who is leaving the faith." Saying it out loud brought tears into her voice, and she swallowed hard against them.

"Ah...." The word came out more like a long sigh. "That's what Elmer thought..."

Nothing could be easily hidden in a family all under the same roof. Maybe it shouldn't surprise her that Ankel Elmer had figured it out.

"So the problem is that Elmer offered him a job, and he's leaving the faith, right?" Trish said. "Should I tell Elmer to take that job offer back?"

"No, no..." Miriam sighed. "It's more than that, honestly. My marriage to Elijah was just one hard day after another. He gambled away all of our money. He left me with nothing. And I mean it—nothing. There's nothing in the bank, and I'd brought a pretty respectable nest egg with me that I'd been saving ever since I started working part-time jobs. He wouldn't listen to me. He ruined us, and all I could do was stand there and watch it happen. The problem is, Aent Trish, I don't want to get married again. I love Zaac—I really do—but even if he were staying Amish, I'm not handing my life over to a man again. I deserve some stability, and happiness, and provisions that I can count on. I deserve to be treated with respect!"

"Many, many women have come to that conclusion," her *aent* said softly. They stopped on the sidewalk, and Aent Trish met Miriam's gaze. "You've been through a lot, and I don't blame you for a moment, especially since marriage as you've known it left you completely powerless. Do you love him?"

"Yah." Tears misted her eyes.

"Then there are other things you can do, you know. There are solutions."

"I want to build my own business," Miriam said. That would provide for her, and she could finally stop worrying about where the money for groceries would come from, or what she would do if her garden didn't produce as well as she needed it to.

"Excellent. But I meant about a marriage relationship."

Miriam eyed her *aent* uncertainly. "We're Amish, Aent Trish. There are certain ways we do things."

Aent Trish shrugged. "There is something I've learned over the years being married to your ex-Amish uncle. I had expectations of what marriage would be like, and he was raised with completely different ideas from a completely different culture. We had to sit down, put aside all of our expectations, and sort out what our marriage would look like. There is the perfect ideal in your head of how a marriage should be, and then there is the reality of how you sort out a marriage with a real live man. They are two very different things, my dear."

"Did you give up some of your hopes?" Miriam asked.

"I let go of some of my pictures of what a marriage should look like," she said. "And so did he. And then we looked at the two of us and what we each needed. We started there, and we decided on a few things that we'd promise each other. Your uncle promised me that we'd make all our decisions jointly. If we both didn't agree, then the decision wasn't made yet."

"I like that…" Miriam said. She'd never heard of something like that before.

"And I promised him that I'd always put our family

first, and that we'd never have a drop of alcohol in our home. That mattered to him, and I was happy to comply."

Miriam looked back toward the Black Bonnet Amish Chocolates shop with the pretty black-and-white sign and the sparkling wide window. An Englisher marriage would be nothing like an Amish one. Amish wives were supposed to be quiet and sweet and accommodating. They were supposed to trust.

Maybe she could trust someone like Zaac. He'd listen to her concerns.

"What would you do if you were me?" Miriam asked.

"I can't rightfully say," Trish replied. "I'm afraid to give advice, because I could be wrong…"

"But?" Miriam pressed.

Trish looked down at her feet for a moment, undecided. Then she sighed.

"Well, for starters, did you know that you can have joint bank accounts so that you have just as much access to them as your husband does?" Trish asked.

"Elijah would never have considered that. He had everything in his name."

"But Zaac might be fine with it."

"What else?" Miriam asked.

"Before you get married is the time for serious discussion about how your relationship will run. You'd have to think about what you need to feel secure. Maybe you need some money set aside in your name, just in case. Maybe after a few years, you'll be okay to put it all together again. Maybe you need your job and your own income. Maybe you need to build up your business and have the freedom to do that, separate from your personal finances. That way your business can grow and flourish regardless of what is happening at home."

"This all sounds like I'm counting on things going wrong," Miriam said. "Isn't that a lack of faith?"

"Sometimes we have to set boundaries to protect ourselves. You've learned the hard way that sometimes a man doesn't keep his promise, and you're scared. If Zaac loves you, he'll understand exactly why you're afraid, and he'll be willing to do what it takes to make you feel safe again."

Miriam was silent, considering this. She'd assumed she'd have to go along with the regular Amish ways, the patterns that left her so helpless. Would it be possible to do things differently, all while staying Amish?

"Think about this," Trish said. "If Zaac is as good a man as Elmer believes him to be—and Elmer tends to be a very good judge of character—what if Zaac simply keeps his word? What if you have a partner in the truest sense, and you discuss everything, and you grow together and support each other? What if he never bulldozes you or bullies you? What if he simply respects you and builds a happy life with you where you never get pushed into a corner, ever?"

They turned back, their steps angled toward the shop, but Miriam's head was spinning. *Yah*, what if? Miriam had to face the reality of things, not the way she wanted them to be. She'd already made that mistake with her first marriage—seeing Elijah as the man he could be instead of the man he was. Miriam wanted Zaac to come back as a conservative Amish farmer, and that would never happen, either. Zaac was a different kind of man. He had progressive ideas and convictions, and a very big heart. But he might still find a way home again...in his own way.

And if he found a way...would she be willing to take

that risk? Could they find a way together that made her feel safe again? Because, and she realized this in one heart-crushing rush, she very deeply longed to feel safe enough to marry Zaac Yoder.

Chapter Fourteen

That morning, Zaac worked in the horse barn and then rode out with his brother-in-law Johannes to check on two different herds. Both herds had fared well during the storm, having had some trees to protect them from the worst of it, and being on higher ground.

Soon, Zaac would be working a much larger ranch with Englisher electronics. The cattle didn't scare him; he knew cattle. But the technology was intimidating. How hard would that adjustment be? And would the ranch hands respect him?

Now that the hurdle of the job was achieved, he was nervous and feeling a nagging sense of regret. He'd chased this down, taken advantage of every opportunity and used what was in his hands… And he'd accepted a job that would change the course of his entire life.

But he'd lost Miriam.

You never had Miriam, he told himself irritably. But he'd held her. He'd kissed her. He'd told her how he felt, and she loved him, too. That was awfully close, wasn't it?

Gott, am I wrong? he prayed for the hundredth time that morning. *Do You have a life for me here in Menno Hills? Would I have Your blessing to marry Miriam?*

At lunchtime, he ate what he could of the meat loaf

sandwiches his *mamm* had made, but he still left half on his plate.

"Isaac, when are you going to see a doctor about that arm of yours?" Mamm asked.

"It's healing," he said.

"Please, just go see Doc Brooks," she said. "I'll feel better once he's looked at it."

So Zaac did what his mother asked and hitched up the buggy and drove into town. He drove past Black Bonnet Amish Chocolates, and everything inside him wanted to stop in, to see Miriam, to get some idea of what she was feeling right now... But he couldn't. She was working. There were appearances to worry about, and it wouldn't be fair of him to carry their messy personal business into her place of work. She had a future, too, and Zaac would not compromise hers.

Zaac went to the medical clinic, waited his turn, and one of the nurses took a look at his arm. They gave him some stitches to close the wound the rest of the way, gave him a little tube of antibiotic ointment, bandaged him back up and sent him on his way.

As he came out of the clinic and started to untie Schon from the hitching post, he noticed Bishop Moses coming by on foot. Funny... He'd dreamed about Bishop Moses when he was sick, and it had felt good to talk to the old man.

"Hello, Isaac," Bishop Moses said, turning his steps in Zaac's direction. "Are you all right?"

"A few stitches, I'll be right as rain," Zaac said. He hadn't meant to draw the bishop's attention, but it looked like he had, after all.

The old man stopped at the side of Zaac's buggy. "You've been wandering around my dreams lately, young man. In one, you were carrying a box for me. In another, you were helping me fix my boot. Just…dreams. But it would seem you are on my mind."

Zaac smiled ruefully. "It would seem. At least I'm helpful in your dreams. I'm glad to hear that."

"Let me pick your brain, Isaac," the bishop said. "I have an Englisher young man about your age who talked with me about an hour ago about getting involved in our church."

Zaac startled. *"Yah?"*

"Yah. And you know as well as I do that drawing him in would be more difficult than simply being friendly."

"I understand the complications," Zaac replied.

"I will confess to you that I have told one local family in the past that they would be better served finding an Englisher church to attend, and I was going to tell this young man the exact same thing, but something stopped me. It felt…wrong to send him away."

"Is his name James Hiebert?"

"The one and the same! You know him?"

"I met him during the storm. We rescued his dog. He's very interested in our ways, Bishop."

"But interest, curiosity…those pass. He can attend a service. He can come to a hymn sing. It would take about that much to convince him that we're duller than tree stumps to his English sensibilities."

"And yet, you haven't told him no," Zaac said.

"No, I haven't," the bishop replied. "This time, I'm considering it. And I'm not sure why."

An abandoned newborn baby, a half-drowned kitten, a wounded dog and his brother's widow… All bound together in one storm, all needing something from Zaac and all brought right to him. And now a young Englisher man feeling drawn to the Amish world. He could feel Gott's hands on this, and while he could never claim to know what Gott was doing, he could feel that He was up to something!

"He'll need someone to take him under his wing and show him the Amish ways," Zaac said.

The bishop's eyebrows went up. "*Yah*, he would."

Someone would need to take responsibility for him. Someone would need to sacrifice his time and energy to show him the Amish life, to show him how to get along, to teach him the language. If James was drawn to the Amish faith, perhaps that was because Gott was leading him to it.

"It's an awful lot to ask of anyone," Bishop Moses said, shaking his head. "I don't know why this particular young man has lodged himself into my mind the way he has, but sometimes Gott brings people into our paths for a reason."

Gott most assuredly brought people together for a reason…but something had occurred to Zaac.

"Bishop, what if someone were willing to be his friend, to accompany him to our services and translate when he needs it? What if someone gave him language lessons, and culture lessons, and, and…" Zaac's thoughts were tumbling out faster than his words could keep up, but he could see it in his mind's eye. The Amish did have something wonderful, unique and truly special. People came to them, looking for the difference. Their very lives were walking sermons! And they could share their faith, so long as someone devoted himself to teaching.

"So you're willing?" the bishop asked.

"Me?"

"I thought you were volunteering. Aren't you?"

And suddenly, it was like all those prayers he'd sent up had just blossomed into his answer. He could feel it in his heart. Maybe Gott's call to spread his love hadn't been to go far from home. Maybe Gott was bringing that mission field right to his door!

"I think I am, Bishop," Zaac said nodding. "I'd like to help him."

"I was right not to send him away. *Danke*, Isaac." The older man cocked his head to one side. "You know, there is the business of your own baptism."

If Zaac was staying, then he knew that he'd need to take that final commitment of baptism—there was no question about that now—but something else had finally clicked into place in his heart. If Gott was asking him to be a missionary from home, then maybe there was a very good reason Gott hadn't wiped Miriam out of Zaac's heart. Gott had brought him Miriam in that storm, too. Right to his heart and into his arms.

"There is the business of my baptism," Zaac said. "But I'm going to have to talk to you about that later, if that's okay. There's something I need to do first…and then, Bishop, I will need to get myself properly baptized, and I will tell you everything."

The bishop smiled and shook his head. "That sounds *gut* to me, my boy!"

Because it had all become clear to Zaac. His *mamm* had been right—there was a life for him right here in Menno Hills, and there was an important job to do that involved bringing others into their fold. Gott was calling him, and he suddenly saw how vast and deep and important this job was. But this calling was at home, and he was filled with such gratitude for that simple fact that he could almost cry. He'd been willing to go to the ends of the earth, but Gott was bringing his mission field to him.

Now to talk to Miriam. Because if she loved him like he loved her, the way had just opened up…for him at, at least. And he wanted to take on this new challenge with the woman he loved at his side.

Was there any chance that she'd take a leap and marry him?

A lineup of customers had formed in Black Bonnet Amish Chocolates. Today was busy, and tourists and locals alike had been coming for Esther Mae's fine chocolates. Miriam slid two boxes of assorted chocolates into a handled paper bag and rang up the order. The Englisher woman paid and gave her a smile.

"Thank you so much. Have a great day," the woman said.

"You, too. Take care," Miriam said.

The next customer in line was a middle-aged man. He had a bundle of roses tucked under one arm, and when Miriam cast him a smile he said, "I'm going to level with you, miss, I'm taking my wife out on a date. Today is the anniversary of our first date. We always celebrate that. What chocolates do you recommend for a woman who loves everything milk chocolate and particularly loves strawberries?"

With the storm over, people seemed to be making up for lost time. And she was noticing how unique people were. Like this man—celebrating the anniversary of a first date. She'd never heard of that, but she could imagine how meaningful that was to his wife. People found ways that worked for them.

She helped the man find a box of cream-filled chocolates that Miriam felt sure his wife would enjoy and rang up his purchase. The bell above the door tinkled again and when she looked up, her heart skipped a beat.

Zaac stood there, his straw hat a little askew and his dark gaze meeting hers. She had three customers ahead of him, though. More chocolate purchases—a grandmother getting some chocolates for a birthday party, a young woman ordering some chocolate centerpieces for a wedding shower. And when the last customer left, Zaac was alone, standing in front of her till. He had his hands in his pockets, a hesitant, hopeful look on his face.

"Hi," he said.

"Zaac..."

"I missed you," he said quietly. "I'll leave if you want me to, but—"

"I missed you, too." Miriam came around the counter, and he caught her fingers in his.

"Look, I know when we last talked everything looked impossible," Zaac said. "But something has changed for me, and I don't know if it will change anything for you, but I had to tell you about it anyway."

"What do you mean, something changed?" she asked.

"I want to marry you."

His words were so simple that they slipped under all her defenses, and she blinked at him. "How?"

"Okay, that's not the order I wanted to say this," Zaac said, color flooding his face. "The thing is, I'm not leaving. I'm staying. I knew Gott was calling me to help others, and I thought I'd have to do that far from here, but Gott has been bringing everything to me, here. I don't know why that surprised me so much. But it did. James wants to join the Amish church, so the bishop needs someone who is willing to teach him our culture, our language, everything. So I said yes. And I'm making my choice for the church. I'm getting baptized.

"I was so certain I had to leave Menno Hills to help Englishers who wanted what we have, but Gott just keeps putting those who need me right into my path. I've been thinking about it and praying about it, and then the bishop asked me to help James learn about our faith, and it all just clicked for me. My mission field is right here."

"I thought you had a job with my *ankel*—"

"I'll have to apologize to him, but I'm not leaving, Miriam. I'm getting baptized. And… I was hoping that when I get baptized, you might be willing to live this unorthodox life with me…as my wife."

Tears sprang to her eyes. "I do love you, Zaac."

"Here's the thing," he said earnestly. "I truly think I need to help people here. Englishers, Amish. Everyone. If you marry me, we'd be helping James learn about the faith, and I don't know what else. But it will be…a different path than you might be expecting. We'll be Amish—I can promise you that. But we'll be helping people join us instead of keeping them out."

A different path…

"I'd need to do things differently, too," Miriam said. "I want to build my own business, and I need to know that you'll treat me like a true partner, that we'd make every single decision together, that you wouldn't railroad me into your way of doing things."

"Of course! Miriam, I will never bully you. I haven't yet, and I will not start."

"And I was thinking about the things that scare me and the things I'd need to feel safe again in a marriage…"

"What do you need?"

"I have a few ideas," she said. "But I'd want to talk about it more before banns are announced or anything like that. I'd have to be sure."

"Miriam, whatever you need, okay? We'll work it out."

She looked down at his hand clasping hers. "But I have a request of my own…if you were to marry me."

"Yah?" he asked hopefully.

"I want to adopt Ivy, Zaac." She lifted her gaze to meet his. "I love her. I want to raise her Amish and show her how precious she is to us and to Gott and to the whole community. I want to have our own *kinner*, and I want to be open to adopting others who need a loving *mamm*. You feel called to help the Englishers. I feel called to be a mother..."

"And you want to start with Ivy," Zaac said, his gaze softening. "*Yah*, Miriam. I'd love that."

"Really?" She just wanted to hear it again, because those words were exactly what she needed to hear.

"Let's get married," he said. "And let's bring Ivy home. She feels like ours already, doesn't she?"

Miriam nodded. "*Yah*. And you feel like mine, Zaac."

Zaac lifted her fingers to his lips, and a clatter made them both pull back. Miriam's cheeks grew warm when she spotted Esther Mae in the doorway to the kitchen, a pan on the floor at her feet.

"Just for clarity," Esther Mae said. "You two are getting married, *yah*?"

Miriam looked up at Zaac, and he nodded.

"*Yah*. We're getting married," he said, his voice deep and certain, and Miriam's heart tumbled in response.

It felt wonderful to hear it out loud, and terrifying, too, and Esther Mae joyfully ran over to where they stood and hugged them both at once.

"Your secret is safe with me until the banns are announced," Esther Mae said, eyes glittering with happiness. "Oh, I knew it! I knew it! I knew if you two just had a little bit of time together, you'd see what I saw!"

There were so many details to take care of, plans to make and agreements to come to as they discussed the serious business of the rest of their lives, but the ones that mattered most right now were marrying Zaac and bringing Ivy home. This was the start of a family, formed in the middle of a storm with the fingerprints of Gott.

Outside the window, a mist of rain started to fall in the middle of the sunny afternoon, and a rainbow flickered into view. It was a full bow, colors blending into colors, and Miriam's heart skipped a beat. Finally, after all she'd endured, she could hear Gott's unmistakable voice in her heart whispering, *Peace. Be still.*

Her storm was past.

Epilogue

Zaac and Miriam had some long, earnest discussions as they rode together in Zaac's buggy. They talked about finances, and *kinner*, and decisions in the home. They made promises to each other about how they would handle disagreements and how they would make sure that Miriam had a voice, too. Zaac was glad she was willing to talk about her fears, because then he knew exactly how to make her happy. And that was his prayer—that Miriam would feel happy and protected, and that she'd keep that joyful glow he loved so much.

Bishop Moses agreed that a speedy wedding made the most sense, considering that there was a baby to bring home. Besides, the old man could feel Gott's hands on this union, too, and he wasn't about to try to slow it down.

After Zaac was baptized, Menno Hills pulled together to put on the wedding. The women cooked up food, and the men helped Zaac's mother to prepare the farm for a proper Amish wedding held under a tent set up in the pasture. There was a little bit of extra work, too, as the men pulled together to prepare the baby's bedroom in the little *dawdie* house Zaac and Miriam would be inhabiting on the Yoder family ranch. There was a crib, a changing table and a toybox in one corner. It was filled with cloth diapers, baby blankets, little baby dresses—some made by friends and family, and other items that Miriam had lovingly stitched for a different child who had never made it to her arms... Somehow, holding those little infant dresses in his hands, Zaac knew the depth of love in Miriam's heart, and he was amazed by her all over again. He thanked Gott for the thousandth time that she was actually going to be his wife.

Zaac would always remember their wedding day with the vows they said before Gott and their community. Everyone came, even on short notice. Elmer and Trish were there with their three adult sons, and Elmer bore no hard feelings about Zaac not taking the job after all.

"This is better," Elmer said, clapping him on the shoulder. "I couldn't be happier for you. I wanted you to be my ranch manager, but stepping up as my nephew is even better. Welcome to the family, Zaac."

But it was the day after their wedding, when the families were still cleaning up, that would lodge itself in Zaac's mind as the day they became a family.

The adoption paperwork was complete, and while Miriam and Zaac had visited Ivy often, and she'd been brought for home visits over the last few weeks as they prepared for this event, this would be the very first day that Ivy came home with them as their own daughter. They stood in the social services office side by side, married for exactly one day, their hearts soaring.

"Congratulations, Mom and Dad," Gwen said, and she passed Ivy into Miriam's arms.

Zaac slid an arm behind Miriam's back, and Miriam leaned into his touch as they looked down at their baby girl who was awake and alert, those wide blue eyes searching their faces. She'd grown a lot since the first day she'd arrived on the Black Bonnet doorstep. She was over eight pounds now, and Zaac couldn't help but feel pride in seeing his baby girl thriving.

Ivy was their daughter now. The thought brought a mist of tears to his eyes. This felt right—so very right—and his heart closed around the two of them. Zaac had a family now—not just a wife, but a daughter, too. And he felt a fierce protectiveness surge up inside of him.

"You're coming home, Ivy," Zaac said softly.

"At last…" Miriam whispered, and they shared a relieved smile.

Zaac loved them. Simply and purely. He would provide for them, protect them and make sure they knew that they filled his heart. He was no longer just Isaac Yoder. He was *Honey*, and he was *Daet*.

For Miriam and Ivy, and with Gott to strengthen him, he would move mountains. He could feel it in his bones.

* * * * *

If you liked this story from Patricia Johns,
check out her previous Love Inspired books:

Grave Amish Secrets
Amish Sleigh Bells
Her Pretend Amish Beau

Available now from Love Inspired!
Find more great reads at www.LoveInspired.com.

Dear Reader,

I love chocolate! It's just so comforting and delicious, isn't it? Chocolate cake, chocolate icing, chocolate brownies, hot chocolate, and delicious boxes of chocolates… It's really hard to go wrong if you start with chocolate! This brand-new miniseries circles around an Amish chocolate shop, and I can't wait to surround myself with the wonderful characters and the delicious treats they offer!

If you enjoyed this story, would you do me a favor? If you'd post a review somewhere telling others that you loved it, it helps to get the word out, and I'd be eternally grateful!

Come find me on social media or pop by my website at patriciajohns.com. I love hearing from my readers, and I'm sure to reply.

Patricia